Cloud of Doubt
James Herman

Order this book online at www.trafford.com
or email orders@trafford.com

Most Trafford titles are also available at major online book retailers.

Note for Librarians: A cataloguing record for this book is available from Library
and Archives Canada at www.collectionscanada.ca/amicus/index-e.html

Printed in Victoria, BC, Canada.

ISBN: 978-1-4269-1482-9 (sc)

*Our mission is to efficiently provide the world's finest, most comprehensive book publishing
service, enabling every author to experience success. To find out how to publish your book, your
way, and have it available worldwide, visit us online at www.trafford.com*

Trafford rev. 9/18/2009

Trafford
PUBLISHING® www.trafford.com

North America & international
toll-free: 1 888 232 4444 (USA & Canada)
phone: 250 383 6864 ♦ fax: 812 355 4082

CHAPTER ONE

"Modeena, Modeena, you forgot your cigarettes."

Modeena stopped in her tracks. She wasn't going anywhere without her Salem's. She gated her large framed legs in a waddling semi-circle while Danny ran the cigarettes down the walk to her. "Thank you honey chil'," she replied in a hoarse, manly voice.

"You're welcome. Modeena, can I walk down to the tracks with you?"

"Sho' enough, I sho nuff needs some company today." Danny's eyes gleamed. He loved Modeena. She was much more than the housekeeper and nanny. Modenna was the only mother Danny knew; she adored him.

Danny was eight, small for his age, blue eyes, blonde hair and an absolute whirlwind of trouble and mischief. Modeena could tell by the look in his eyes what he was thinking. She was very good at reading eyes. The lower limbs of the peach tree were almost bare from cutting seldom used switches.

Modeena began working for Claude De Moss soon after his wife Evelyn succumbed to breast cancer shortly after Danny's birth. Evelyn De Moss had noticed a lump in her breast. A variety of doctors, specialists and treatments did not stop the deliberate gradual progression of the destruction to her body. She became pregnant between treatments of radiation and chemotherapy, one of the peaks on the roller coaster of her health history.

Evelyn was filled with excitement and hope for the future. She had heard of other women winning the battle. The doctors wanted to perform a mastectomy, actually urged her. They warned her the cancer cells would spread. The pregnancy was complicated, but radiation and chemotherapy would harm the baby. Choices would have to be made, none of them good, mastectomy, abortion, or have the baby, suspending treatment temporarily. She opted for suspending treatments, a gamble, a deadly gamble.

Danny was born on February 14, 1956. Her Valentine, the love of her life. A part of Claude and herself that would carry on, their gift to the world. The birth weakened Evelyn. She was sent home for a short time with the baby only to return to long delayed treatments. She died April 14, 1956.

Claude would have died of a broken heart if God had not sent him Modeena. She nurtured him, encouraging him not to give up on life. In the early days of mourning she would simply place a hand on his shoulder and say, "Mr. Claude, everthin' gonna be alright, it just take time."

Modeena was right. Slowly Claude thought less about Evelyn although every hour of every day he knew in his heart she was the love of his life and there would never be another.

Danny was spoiled by Claude. He seldom offered any discipline or raised his voice. That was Modeena's job. Modeena was an old school, down south black momma, so things balanced nicely. When Modeena went off she meant business. Claude would simply raise his newspaper or go into another room, anything not to interfere with Modeena's black wrath. Claude knew it was best, and that Modeena wouldn't harm Danny. He also knew he couldn't do it. A push over when it came to Danny. Mostly he knew Modeena was just what Danny needed.

Claude had grown to love and trust Modeena. A very special unfailing anchor to both of them.

Modeena stopped at the end of Sayle Street where the tracks crossed.

"Mr. Danny, dis here is as far as you can go. Dees big ol' trains is dangerous. Dey ain't gotz no brakes. No sir, none at all."

Danny turned and made a bee line back toward his house. Modeena had terrified him, just as she had intended. Modeena was amused as she watched him run, holding his straw hat with one hand and his toy six shooter in the other. One of the trains let out an ear shattering whistle. Danny ran even faster, letting go of his hat and gun. Suddenly his hat blew off. He looked down at his PF flyers sliding across the loose gravel on the side of the road. Quickly he retrieved his hat and in no time was at full gallop again.

Modeena watched until he made the turn through the gate of the white picket fence that circumscribed the white, two story house. Modeena let out a laugh, shook her head, spoke aloud to herself as she often did, "Gaud damn, dat boy can run."

Modeena ambled across the switching yard, multiple tracks where box cars were coupled together to make trains. Once trains they departed east to Florida or west toward Texas, far from the heart of the Mississippi delta. Hobos, tramps, and vagabonds gathered at the switching yard, a union station for the dirt poor and down trodden.

On frequent occasions they made their way to the De Moss house for handouts. They had a mysterious knack for knowing which houses to visit. Modeena told Danny they had a secret code among them, marking certain houses for free-loading. If Danny wasn't at school he would watch from the screened back porch as Modeena would fetch them bologna sandwiches and ice water. Modeena never sent a one of them away hungry. She was a soft touch, Danny had seen enough to gain that insight. Her disguise was a very hard outer shell.

The spring and summer months brought the season of begging and panhandling into full bloom. It started with a banging of the screen door on the back porch. Modeena answered, immediately she recognized the first of many to come in the summer of 1964.

He was of average height, slight build, and spoke with an accent from up north, somewhere cold Modeena figured.

"Mam, could I impose on you for something to eat? I haven't had a bite in three days."

Modeena eyed him from head to foot. His hair was long and uncombed, a stubbled beard surrounded his worn face. Dusty clothes were dirty and oversized, no doubt a handout. You could smell him long before Modeena opened the door.

"You stays right here, don't go messin' with nothin'!"

Modeena made him two sandwiches, that is she brought him four pieces of white bread and four slices of bologna.

She held it out to him in one hand, the bread with the bologna on top. Then the sermon began, "God helps dose dat helps demselves."

The hobo sat quickly on the concrete steps that lead to the upper concrete porch, and began building the sandwiches. Modeena was seven or eight steps above him. He was her one man congregation.

"Gaud damn, why don't you get a job? I swear you don't has to be no tramp. Dey is always a job down to the flour mill. Loadin'dem box cars with dem heavy sacks of flour." Then she would point to the tallest cylindrical structures in town. The mill was fairly nearby, within walking distance. With that the stranger left while still tearing away at his sandwiches. Rudeness and nagging Modeena knew would send them on their way. The conversations were one-sided, loud and terse.

"I ain't got no patience wiff yo' kind. Don't come back here no mo', and I do mean no mo'!"

Danny found the encounters amusing. He knew Modeena was nothing like the act she put on, to Danny it was entertainment. Sometimes, after quietly watching the performance, he would make smart aleck comments.

"Are you out of bologna yet?" or "I think that one liked you Modeena."

Danny always smiled his crooked, smirking little smile. He could see right through her and Modeena knew it. They both laughed.

Every night except Saturday night Modeena stayed the night at the De Moss house. In the mornings Claude took Danny to school. Modeena would cross the tracks to her one room shack, just to check to see if anyone had been "messin'wif'it." Sometimes out of the blue she would spend a night or two, maybe three, there. As if to ground herself in her real world.

The place was run down and depressing. Claude couldn't figure why she bothered. The unpainted grayed wood somehow seemed to fit the lopsided walls and undulating moss stained roof. Inside the floors had slats missing and gently curved over each support. Old newspapers were stuffed into cracks in the walls. Modeena would strip a small piece of newspaper to start a fire in the soot covered wood burning stove which was also the only source of heat. Modeena recalled salvaging the rust stained sink on one of her excursions to the local dump.

Claude had been inside once. He asked Modeena why she needed a sink without water.

"I just fills it with da water hose."

Claude replied by saying, "I take it there is no water heater?"

"Mr. Claude, if'in I needs hot water, I heats me some on dat stove."

The outhouse was fairly close to the house. In the summertime the flies were bothersome. Many times Modeena would "hold it" until she got to the De Moss'.

Modeena was born in 1929. Mules were used in the cotton fields back then. Modeena had worked those fields all her life. She praised the Lord when Mr. De Moss had picked her from the back of a pickup truck loaded with field hands. She often wondered why Mr. Claude had chosen her. Was it because she was about the same age as his wife would have been?

At first, when Modeena started working in the house she dusted a lot. Mr. Claude had said, "Modeena, I don't expect you to dust everyday, but I'd appreciate you dusting off that wedding picture every day."

Modeena got to where she studied every detail. She loved the photo. Mr. Claude was so young and handsome, "similin', showin' off every toof'. Evelyn was beautiful. Instinctively she knew how different she was from them: white, educated, trim. Black, no schoolin', large, but a pretty glowing face. Modeena was always happy, except when she was acting in the backyard. Even then she was happy inside.

There was a rhythm to her, in everything she did, her walk, her voice, the blues and gospel songs she sang. Half sung, half hummed, a slow deep, melodic, mellow sound.

Most nights she read her dog-eared Bible. Sometimes when she had trouble with the big words, Mr. Claude would help her out, although she astonished him. A self-taught reader and serious student of the bible. Claude wondered if she'd had an education, a different start to her life, what would she be? Where would she be? He was thoroughly convinced, anything, anywhere she wanted.

Modeena's only fault, if it was a fault, was her language. "Gaud damn" was ingrained in her speech, along with other choice words. Claude overlooked it, and never attempted to correct her. He knew there was an unshakeable love and trust in God in her heart.

Modeena attended an all black church where marathon services began on Sunday mornings and ran well into the afternoon. Modeena and her best friend, Artie Mae, sang in the choir and feverishly worshiped the Lord. They were good people. God-fearing, fun-loving, and lord did Artie Mae and Modeena love to dress up in their finest Sunday bests. It was the social event and highlight of their week.

Claude was also a regular church goer. He and Evelyn had joined shortly after their marriage. Both had vowed to raise Danny in the church and he attended along with his Dad. A year or so after Evelyn's passing church members tried to fix Claude up with the small number of available women. None of them seemed even close to a match. Each time he met someone new, he just could not bring himself to ask her out. His thought always turned to Evelyn, how much he had loved her. Besides, new people in Elmbrook were few and far between, women of any interest were taken. Little did Claude know that was about to change.

CHAPTER TWO

Claude kissed Danny goodbye and gave Modeena the number to
the hotel in New Orleans. Claude had been there before on business.
He usually stayed in his room. His normal routine was to sit down
with the overseas shipping brokerage people for next year's shipping
contracts and leave the following day. Every year was the same;
smoke, brandy, just a little ass-kissing and minor negotiations. The
shipping prices were per bale of cotton and a few cents one way or
the other could make a substantial difference in his annual income.
Big business? No, but mighty important to Claude. After all, his
business and Danny were all he had.

9:00 AM Cooley Cotton Company. Claude was right on time
as usual. He half-way dreaded these annual meetings, but it was the
only chance he had to improve his bottom line. The giant mahogany
double doors with their ornate brass hardware were before him. As
he pulled on the door he felt a tug, released it knowing someone was
on the other side. The moment he saw her his face turned ashen
white, for longer than a second he was face to face with Evelyn. It
couldn't be! His mind knew Evelyn was gone. But at that moment
his mind could not catch up fast enough.

Finally he said, "Hello, I'm Claude De Moss," slightly embarrassed
by the trick his mind had played on him.

His attention immediately shifted to Neal Bushard, the man he
had been cutting deals with for ten or more years. Neal was Mr.
Cooley's son-in-law. Cooley was semi-retired and spent most of his

time duck hunting in the winter, golfing and off-shore fishing in the spring and summer. A multi-millionaire many times over, but his heart was still in trading and brokering cotton. Everywhere he went, he had up-to-date access to the cotton market. He popped into the office once or twice a week to check the ticker tape. Cooley knew from his early years how vital it was to stay on top of the market. Big money could change hands in a matter of hours. The Cooley Cotton Company actually bought the cotton from intermediate companies like Claude De Moss' cotton compress. Claude bought it from the cotton gin with help from the First National Bank. Local farmers harvested it from the fields and sold it at the gin. The whole deal was like a poker game. The farmers took all the chances; land, seed, constantly spraying for various insects, and most importantly, the weather. Drought, no cotton. Too much rain, it would rot in the field from root rot or just be physically beaten to the ground. The government set the price a few cents above what it cost to produce, barring natural disaster.

Claude knew the farmers were the real risk takers and did all the work. He respected them and liked almost all of them. Secretly he wanted to be a farmer but most of the farms were inherited. Family to family, generation to generation. Claude had not been that lucky. City folk thought a farmer in bib overalls and a big chew of tobacco was some kind of moron. Locals knew better. The dirtiest and most bedraggled were often the best farmers and made nice sums of money if they had a good crop.

Claude rarely drank anything stronger than sweet tea. Tonight with the mystery woman on his mind he stopped by the hotel bar. The bartender had already served him four double bourbons, straight up. His thoughts could not be stopped. Who was she? How could she so closely resemble Evelyn? Why could he not stop thinking about her? He ordered another double, the bartender slid him the rest of the bottle.

"Hey mister, I don't know your troubles. Take this back to your room. I'll put it on your bill. I see the pain in your eyes. Been there myself."

Claude, not at all sober, made his way to the elevator. He took a couple more swigs from the bottle on the way up to room 1430, his room.

While fumbling for his keys, the door across the hall, room 1431, opened.

Claude stood in stunned silence. She made her way toward him. "My name is Clara. I thought we knew each other today. Perhaps in another life."

"Maybe. No, I don't think so. I was just taken aback. You look so much like my late wife Evelyn. I was so surprised, dumbfounded, actually."

Clara smiled, "So, you're a widower?"

"Yes, eight years now."

"I would say, let's go have a drink, but it looks like you got an early start. Let me help you with your key," Clara replied.

2:00 AM Clara cracked the door to Claude's room open. She peeked right, then left. Quickly she made her way across the hall to her room. It was a night to remember she thought as she pulled back the sheets to the bed in her room. The second time she had done so tonight.   Claude's eyes opened. Groggy, his head spinning slightly, "Oh shit, I can't lift my head off the pillow," he thought.

What the hell happened last night? Was it real or was it a dream?

No, it wasn't a dream. Her name is Clara La Salle. She's from Mobile, Alabama and she does the same thing I do. She was here to contract her cotton. She poured the bourbon down the sink and helped me to bed. I was drunk alright, but not enough to pass out, just enough to talk too much. Way too much. I can't believe the things I said to her. How strikingly beautiful she looked. Even the shape of her face had stunned him, it was a perfect match. Down to her shoulder length blonde hair, the full perky lips, a flawless complexion, but most of all the eyes. A deep mystic blue, he had only seen once before. Did I tell her about Evelyn? Yes, hell yes! Gaud dammit! What a fool, what a fool I made of myself. She must think I am some drunken idiot!

No, I told her I didn't usually drink that much. Did she believe me? Yes, she wetted a washcloth and put it on my head, over my eyes. I cried. Oh shit, I cried! I told her how much I loved Evelyn. How I still missed her terribly. Gaud dammit! Gaud dammit!

She kept saying, "We'll talk about it in the morning...at breakfast, at 10 AM."

Gaud dammit, gaud dammit. What time is it? Ten after ten. Oh shit!

Claude walked into the crowded hotel dining room. Claude thought, "Shit, she's gone." It was 10:35.

No, in the corner, there she was. Claude approached sheepishly. Damn this is going to be awkward.

Clara turned, a big beautiful smile. Their eyes met, it was electric.

Electrons, magnetism, totally invisible, yet it was there, man was it there!

Claude just stood there, half hypnotized. They gazed at each other for a good ten seconds or more. Finally Clara reached out for his hand. She held it gently. Claude felt a rush. My God, how I miss that. Surprised by his lack of human touch, no, it was more than that, a female touch.

Claude felt he held on too long. A man stranded in the desert finally finding water. He could not drink enough or fast enough. His soul's thirst was finally drinking.

Claude's mind caught up, snapped back to real time. There was a glass of orange juice on the table obviously ordered by Clara.

"Thought you could use that," Clara replied.

Claude looked at it. His mind drifted again. When had anyone, beside Modeena done that?

"How do you feel this morning?"

"Okay, considering. Did... did anything happen last night?"

"No, but it wasn't from your lack of trying. You went through a short octopus phase. But mostly you were sweet."

The waitress appeared, "Can I take your order?"

Their eyes never left each other as they placed their orders.

The waitress could see it. Hell anyone, everyone could see it. Sparks were flying!

The waitress smiled, she was standing within the glow.

Clara and Claude talked for over an hour.

Clara's husband had been one of the first pilots killed in Vietnam, a Marine Lieutenant. They had been high school sweethearts, attended the University of Alabama together. Lt. Taylor Bruce La Salle was his name. Clara worked for her father-in-law and his brother. La Salle Brother's Cotton, one of the biggest in the south.

Clara had a business degree majoring in marketing. Taylor had majored in agriculture, but spent his summer's crop dusting. Taylor's dad and uncle were flyers in World War II. Bob, Taylor's Dad, flew fighters in the Pacific and Dick flew B-17 bombers over Germany. Both were accomplished businessmen; expert cotton traders and pilots.

The family took Taylor's death hard. His mother took it hardest, very hard. With the loss of Taylor, her only son, she became an outright drunkard.

Marie had ordered a case of Vodka each month for twenty-five years. Entertaining, socializing with family and friends, they used it up with a bottle or two to spare.

Now Marie was ordering a case a week, not eating and getting worse by the day. The friends and family, and entertaining were gone. Somehow in her depressed state that seemed okay. Only a year ago that seemed impossible, she loved to socialize, surrounded by friends and family. She missed the parties, mostly she missed the evenings when Bob, his brother Dick, and Dick's wife Trudy would gather at her house around the pool patio. They would have a few drinks; laugh and share local gossip, and generally cut up. They truly had a good time. Enjoying each others company immensely. But now she was living in hell on earth. Bob was a wreck himself and understood Marie's pain. They were both devastated, but Bob had a business to run. For six months he didn't follow the market and showed up at work with the intention of working all day, only to leave after a couple of hours. Bob worked his way to eight hour days, he was better, but not recovered enough to help Marie.

Clara looked in on Marie every day around noon. Peculiarly, Clara was holding up the best. She put Marie to bed to sleep it off, tried to get her to eat something when she awoke. They mostly cried and hugged. She begged Marie to slow down on the Vodka. Nothing was working.

"Why don't you call the liquor store and stop the deliveries?" Claude asked.

"Well, she owns it, along with several other local businesses. Actually, she's the money and the brains behind all the family businesses, including La Salle Cotton."

"Bob is picking me up in his plane at the airport at three o'clock. I need to leave."

"Can I drive you?"

"No, that wouldn't be a good idea. I don't think Bob is ready to see me with another man. You understand, don't you?"Clara asked.

"When can I see you again? Can I phone you?"When will you be back in New Orleans?" Claude was beginning to panic.

Clara hesitantly gave Claude her number, walked around the table and took his hands in hers. They kissed a long deep kiss. She couldn't believe the way he made her feel.

Mixed emotions were bubbling over, excitement, fear, exhilaration, along with apprehension, trepidation. Love? Guilt?

Claude was driving back to Mississippi later the same day. He thought about going back to the hotel, but the thought of Clara not being there, depressed him. He let his mind wander into the future. What if Clara moved in with him? How would Danny feel about it? Modeena? Hell, I haven't even had a date with her.

Will she see me again? She never answered my question. Why didn't she? There must be a reason. I can understand her allegiance and loyalty to the La Salle's. They love her. Hell, they employ her.

What is her life in Mobile like?

Does she have someone else?

CHAPTER THREE

Clara and Bob landed in Mobile.

"We'll see you at the office tomorrow," Bob said as he put her suitcase in the trunk of her new red Mercedes roadster. Clara dropped the top even though it was nearing sundown. She loved her car, a gift for her birthday from the LaSalle's.

Fact was, Taylor was always pampered. Cars, clothes, boats, planes; anything his heart desired. Clara was very comfortable with her lifestyle. When she first took an interest in Taylor, part of the appeal was the family money. The icing on the cake was he was handsome, smart and witty, but the money was definitely the "cake." Clara sped away, she was in a hurry. Twelve miles north of Mobile, at the end of a slow "S" curve, Clara braked hard. She had checked her rear view mirror and saw no one. A hard right turn on a red dusty sand road, two more miles, another hard right, the lane was just two tracks where tires had created a road. Ahead, headlights flashed on then off. Clara felt her heart beating faster, flushed, her eyes narrowed and flashed. Again she checked 360 degrees around her. The coast was clear. She leapt from her Mercedes and ran to the idling 4 X 4 pick-up. She climbed in, ripping at her blouse while sliding across the seat.

She had missed Cliff. He had been taking care of her needs shortly after Taylor left for overseas. The tryst, rendevous, and raw sex was exciting, addictive. Clara felt no guilt, the exhilaration alone blocked that.

There was no conversation, they had done this many times before kissing, groping, and the main course.

The twosome had this down. Cliff wore sweat pants and a Crimson Tide t-shirt; quick easy access to what Clara wanted. The sweats made a hasty exit possible if need be. Cliff was a large man, chiseled rock hard, a rough stubbled beard, dark brown eyes, and short crew cut hair. Handsome in a way. Not the sharpest knife in the drawer; closer to a spoon.

Cliff was a part-time bartender, and full time graduate student. He was working on his masters in physical education, had plans to teach at the junior college level. His interests were young women and how many times he could go back to back.

His wife and two young daughters didn't see him much. Too busy, much too busy.

Clara slowly approached the highway, lights out, looking for the glow of any traffic from the highway.

Ok, clear.

Clara pulled back onto the highway; back toward Mobile.

A few deep breaths of salty night air. She felt guilty now. She told herself she wouldn't do it again. This was the last time. She knew she was lying to herself.

Satisfied, she daydreamed into the darkness. Claude was nice, sweet, the way he made her feel. Special, very special she thought. Maybe love was in the future.

Cliff was rough, manly, knew what he wanted and went right after it. There was never a romance. She liked it rough sometimes. All she knew was she amused herself with Cliff. He started flirting with her at the Country Club bar, in fact, Cliff flirted with every woman that came in there. Hell, Cliff even flirted with Marie.

Clara remembered Maria telling her the first time she met him. This guy is the horniest man alive. Rumor is he is very blessed below the belt. Clara laughed by the way Marie said it. She even wondered if Marie had succumbed to his lewd comments, and bleach white teeth. Cliff was a woman's man alright, always on the verge of stepping over the line. He was a master at his craft, backing off instantly at the first sign his charms were being wasted. Surprisingly, Cliff found most women love to flirt. It made them feel attractive, sexy, wanted by the opposite sex. He knew there was no such thing as a harmless flirtation, to him only opportunity was knocking, the louder the better.

Clara rounded a curve on the outskirts of Mobile, she could see the derrick cranes used to unload ships in the distance. Her eyes focused on their lights, her mind drifted further back in time. Back to Taylor, the love of her life. She could never remember him being rough with her, not even once. He was a nice, sweet man, like Claude, she thought. How much their personalities matched, Claude even spoke in the same tone of voice. Their mannerisms, the way they walked, were almost identical. She thought more about Taylor, tears came to her eyes, they did truly love each other, but Taylor was dead.

Sunday morning. Claude was getting ready for church, as he stepped out of the shower the phone rang. He twisted a towel around himself and raced to the phone. Trailing large droplets of water, he stood in a small puddle on the hardwood floor. He hoped it was Clara.

"Hi Claude, it's Clara."

Claude made a fist of victory. Composing himself as best he could, "I was hoping it was you. I see you got back to Mobile in one piece. Those small planes kinda scare me."

"Oh, we fly almost everywhere we go. You get used to it."

"Yeah, guess so," Claude said thinking his station wagon needed tires. This gal is out of my league, he thought. She could never be happy with me in Elmbrook.

"I'm going to be at the Baker Hotel in Memphis in two weeks. Any way you can get free?"

"I'll be there. What day? What time?" Claude said as he realized he was talking too fast.

"It's a business trip, so Bob will drop me at the airport Friday afternoon. Can you meet me in the lobby around 7:00?" Clara replied.

"Yes, I'll be there."

Claude was restless the next two weeks. His concerns growing about Clara's different lifestyle. Nevertheless, he began planning their first date, Beale Street, home of the Blues, a romantic smoky tavern. He would need to find the best restaurant in Memphis.

Modeena had noticed Claude was happier, a certain spring in his step. He even told a joke at dinner, then announced he was going to Memphis for the weekend. Modenna knew something was brewing. Claude only left Elmbrook once a year for the New Orleans contracts.

Friday finally arrived. Claude worked until 10:00 AM and headed for Memphis. On the way Claude wondered should he get a room when he arrived?

The lobby of the Baker Hotel was more than Claude was expecting. Much better than anywhere he had been. Claude was anxious, the high ceiling, chandelier, and eloquent french provincial furniture made him feel out of place. The distraction was welcome, Clara was late. It was 7:15. He tugged at the tie he seldom wore.

Clara emerged from the entry lobby. Her yellow sun dress draped around her shoulder accented her blonde hair, blue eyes, and fair, perfect complexion. She approached Claude speechless, took his hand and placed it against her cheek, then kissed it softly.

"Be back in a minute. Wait here." Clara said

Clara went to the concierge, checked in, and returned to Claude. "We're in the penthouse suite."

Claude was surprised by the eloquence of the suite and at Clara's boldness.

Clara poured herself and Claude a drink. As she handed Claude the drink she declared, "Let the weekend begin."

Beale Street, drinks, dinner, making love the entire weekend. It was the extension of what began in New Orleans.

Claude was exhausted. He and Clara agreed to meet once a month. Claude was falling in love.

CHAPTER FOUR

Six months later
> Baton Rouge, Louisiana
> Shreveport, Louisiana
> Jackson, Mississippi
> Montgomery, Alabama
> Macon, Georgia
> Atlanta Georgia

Clara always chose the places where they would meet. On occasion Claude suggested Myrtle Beach or Fort Lauderdale, some place more romantic. Clara declined, "Honey, I'm working. Expense account, travel, everything is on Cooley Cotton."

"Cooley Cotton, out of New Orleans, I thought you worked for La Salle Brothers in Mobile?"

"I do, but I free lance from time to time."

The places they were going was a mystery to Claude. He was with Clara almost all the time except Saturday afternoons. She would leave the hotel around 10 AM and return in four or five hours. Always with shopping bags, dresses, shoes, and purses. Claude was amazed at the sheer volume of stuff she had packed into his station wagon.

Clara and Claude parted in time for Claude to drive back to Elmbrook. Clara took a cab to the airport to meet Bob.

Claude had never seen Bob. He was becoming concerned; how could Clara afford such lavish, extravagant things. Everything seemed too much, too many. Cooley Cotton was big, but not that big, or was it? LBJ Democrats were escalating the war, that would be a good sign for southern farmers. Democrats got farm subsidies and that was good for Claude's business. Life was good in general, a new woman in his life, business was looking good, the military was beginning to buy huge volumes of cotton goods. Nobody seemed to ask why.

Claude told himself his mind was working overtime. He tried to quell his inner thoughts.

Claude was in love, he was ready to take Clara to Elmbrook. Maybe ask her to marry him. It was very important to Claude that Modeena and Danny liked her. Deep down, Claude could never see Clara fitting into Elmbrook. But his love for her overpowered his thoughts.

Claude also reflected on his money situation. Hell, Clara had bought tires for his station wagon so he could rendevous monthly. Besides Clara would have to refashion her life. Was she willing to do that?

Clara called, Baton Rouge, this weekend. The routine was the same, better than good sex, shopping, the usual departure.

Claude left the hotel at 8 PM plenty of time to get back home before midnight. Around 11 o'clock Claude rounded a slow curve. Then it happened. BLAM! The station wagon tilted, and rolled to a coasting stop. Claude fumbled in the glove compartment for a flashlight, made sure he was positioned far enough off the shoulder of the road, then walked toward the right rear tire.

"Gaud damn flat. I haven't had one of these in a year," Claude said. Actually it was six months to the day before the new tires.

Claude proceeded with exchanging the spare for the flat tire. Finishing up he heaved the flat tire into the cargo compartment. Claude heard a thump after the tire hit the wagon's floor.

"What the hell was that?"

Claude shined his flashlight on what looked like a small bag of flour.

"What is this?" he asked aloud. Claude inspected further, the tire had separated from the rim. Inside were more bags. He fished them out one by one. Ten all together.

Claude stood silently in the stillness. A certain immobility in his entire body. His brain marked time, tranquilized.

Finally, dazed, Claude closed the tailgate and returned to the driver's seat. His hands fixed on the steering wheel, watching as bugs scurried and scrambled in the beams of his own headlights.

Claude knew instinctively what was there, it was bad. He wanted no part of it.

Now the hard part. How did it get there?

Claude drove into the night and thought. I was lucky no one passed by. Is there more? Who did it belong to? Was he in danger? It was sheer luck to have found it? I didn't put it in there. Who did?

Claude's mind lagged. He plodded along, mentally.

Is there more? Probably, I have four tires don't I.

TIRES— CLARA

Who did it belong to? If there's more, it's a drug dealers. More? Hell! I have enough to spend my natural life in prison. Of course it's a dealer, you idiot.

Claude kept talking aloud to himself. Was he in danger? I have a trunk full of some kinda dope, possibly three more tires full.

Shit, shit, shit.

You dumb ass.

It was sheer luck I found it?

Flat tire, I was wondering why those tires never seem to wear out. I ran over something, it was a blowout. Even a new tire can blow out.

I didn't put it there. Who did?

Who drove my car last? CLARA. SATURDAY. She was gone most of the afternoon.

My God, she's used me as a mule.

Clara does not love me.

The mix of emotions was soul stirring; love, betrayal, sadness, anger. Clara had exploited Claude's weakness. His pitiful, almost begging need to be loved. Claude had waited so long for the pain of Evelyn's death to pass. The pain a person never wants to feel.

Claude pulled into the drive. He was home. Modeena had left the porch light on as she always did when he was out after dark. He just sat there, maybe thirty minutes, an hour, two, he didn't know.

"I have to hide this stuff. What will happen if I'm caught? I'm innocent, They would never believe me. I don't believe me."

"No, I'll leave it here until morning."

"I'll call Clara, no, that would be a mistake.

Claude forced himself out of the car. The walk from the drive to the front door seemed endless. Inside, he collapsed into his chair. His brain felt like mush.

"Mr.Claude, Mr.Claude, in all my born days I ain't never seen you sleep in dat chair. Is you alright?" Claude had drifted off shortly before sunrise. Actually his eyes fluttered in and out of a brief fleeting nap. "Mr. Claude what's wrong wiff you, you is grey around da mouth, all da color done lef yo face."

Claude buried his face in his hands and began to cry. He was a good man, he went to church, he loved his family, he was a good provider. How could he have been this stupid? Clara, Clara, he cried a long time. He could feel the blood gushing from his wounded heart.

Modeena put her arm on his shoulder, "Mr. Claude everythin gonna be alright."

Tears rose in Modenna's eyes, as she helped Claude to bed. After she closed the door she wiped them away with her apron. "God is great, please Lord help Mr. Claude."

When Claude awoke from his four hour nap, little did he know how long it would be before he slept another full night. Too much pain, too many thoughts, too disturbed by the turn of events.

Claude had a plan. Half-baked, incomplete, yes. The best a man in his condition could come up with.

The garage cleaning was underway. He had a garage at one time. Now it was full of junk, mostly things of Evelyn's he couldn't throw away. Old toys Danny had outgrown. It took half the day just to make room for the station wagon.

Claude went to the local auto salvage yard, returned with four used tires. He would exchange them for the dope tires. Now the moment of truth, he began to break the tires from the rims with a hammer and chisel. It was a long arduous process. Claude was right, he now had forty bags. There was an old beer cooler among the junk, he got a shovel and placed everything in the back of the wagon and waited for dark to fall.

Claude pulled out cautiously, making sure he wasn't followed. He drove to the compress ware house where he removed part of the floor of the storage area. He sealed the cooler with duct tape, dug and buried the cooler, then replaced the wooden planks. On the return trip he noticed a plain white van trailing. Claude pulled over; it passed. It had no lettering on it.

Modeena had supper on the table. He had forgotten to eat today. His nerves frayed to the bone.

Sleep was a thing of the past. He walked up and down, looking out at the street every ten minutes or so. Imagining all the different themes his situation could take. Claude wrote them in a spiral ring notebook, thinking that will make things more clear.

Theme #1: Clara found him, used him, had no romantic interest in him at all. She was simply using his station wagon to smuggle dope.

Theme #2: Maybe it wasn't Clara. The road goes back and forth to the places he had been. What if someone in Elmbrook placed it. No, doesn't make sense. He was on the return trip to Elmbrook. The dopes destination is Elmbrook. Then why has no one tried to retrieve it? Why hasn't Clara called? She usually calls to see if I made it home safely. Yeah, right.

Theme #3: Maybe it was a mistake. When I got the new tires the installers put them on the wrong vehicle. That was six month's ago, maybe its been there that long. Where did I get the new tires? New Orleans. No, Memphis. Yeah, Memphis.

My first time with the harlot. Invisible steam was rising from his hotheaded ideas.

Theme #4: It can't... can't be Clara. I love her. Maybe she's unaware of the dope. She just wanted us to be together. That's why she bought the tires. But the plane, Bob, shopping, too many coincidences...

Claude saw headlights, then dashed to the window. It was a white van, no lettering, passing by. It seemed slower than regular traffic that passed. He watched another hour, stationed at the window. Sporadic sleep. He needed a drink, but he never kept it at home. Methodist didn't do that in the South.

Morning broke. He was going to work today. Modeena fixed breakfast; ham, eggs, and biscuits. Claude ate half of it. Modeena shook her head, mumbled something to herself as Claude ambled out the door in a daze.

"Good God." Claude, mouth ajar, was looking at the wagon lying flat on the ground. All four tires and rims were gone. He looked right, left, up, down, as if somehow the tires were suspended in air. He ran stumbling, half falling back to the door. His head and eyes fixed on the wagon. Were they still here? They know I have it. The white van, no lettering.

Claude didn't go to work. He called a garage for tires and a tow truck. The wagon was back by noon fit with four more used tires.

That night a call from Neal Bushard wanting to know if he was making the contract negotiations coming up in July. The market was so hot a lot of traders and shippers thought early negotiations were necessary.

Claude said he would be there. Secretly, he suspected everyone knew. After the call he set a theme #5 in his notebook.

Theme #5: Neal Bushard received dope in New Orleans, where it was picked up by Bob and Clara. They then flew it to Baron Rouge, Shreveport, Jackson, Montgomery, Macon, Atlanta where it was further distributed by some unknowing love-struck fool, named Claude.

Hell no, can't be. None of these farmers are using that stuff. The local high school had two arrests for marijuana possession last year. People around here just don't use that stuff. It should be the opposite. No, take it to some little po-dunk town, collect it, and then send it to the bigger cities. Hey, wait a minute. That's it!

Baton Rouge, Shreveport, Jackson, Montgomery, Macon, Atlanta are not big cities, big towns by southern standards. But not New York, Chicago, L.A., Dallas, or Houston.

Carry it a step further, he thought. No major airports, not even a runway long enough to land a Lear jet. The major mode of transportation in Elmbrook is trains, freight trains. Major shippers, the cotton compress and grainary. It's making sense now.

CHAPTER 5

A month passed, it was time to go to New Orleans. Clara had called, she sounded the same as always. Claude was careful not to sound to down. They would meet in New Orleans on Friday morning; do the contracts and stay the weekend.

Claude loaded the wagon with his suitcase. Inside, contained a small vial of the mystery substance. He intended to find someone in New Orleans to analyze it.

Claude arrived, Clara was radiant. They went about their usual affairs. Clara seemed more loving than ever, she almost clung to him. Maybe Claude was putting off some negative vibes. She noticed Claude was not sleeping well, drinking more, and not quite as responsive in the bedroom.

"Is that invitation to Elmbrook open?" Clara said.

"Yes, yes it is," Claude replied.

He didn't want to let go of the hope that she was not involved. Almost instantly he thought she's coming for other sinister reasons.

Saturday afternoon, Clara went shopping. Claude got a taxi right behind her. He asked the driver to take him to a bar on Bourbon Street. The hair stood on the back of his neck.

Hawkers, fortune tellers, watch salesmen, anything for everybody. A young black man approached. "Hey, brother, want some weed? Nickel? Dime?"

"No, what's your name?" Claude asked.

"Rabbit"

Claude produced the vial. "Rabbit, can you help me find out what's in this vial? A hundred dollars is in it for you. Fifty now, fifty later. If you don't come back in an hour I'm leaving with your other fifty dollars."

Rabbit returned. "It's 'H' man, heroin."

"You know for sure?"

"I took it to my man, you know. It's the real deal."

Claude paid him the other fifty. "Where's my vial?:

"You kidden man? My man shot it up, dat's da test. It's some good shit."

Claude returned to the hotel, Clara had not returned.

Claude was restless, more so than usual. He hoped it was a mistake, thought again. How much was what he had worth? How could he sell it?

Sunday at noon Clara said she would like to come see his home, meet Modeena and Danny. Clara knew his life was with them and if she was going to be part of it they had to accept her. Bob would fly her up, she confessed her relationship with Claude to Bob. She wanted them to meet.

Claude was at the airport in Elmbrook on Friday. The small twin engine landed, taxied, and cut his engine. Clara emerged with a big smile, looking as beautiful as ever. Bob followed.

"This is awkward," Clara declared.

"Claude, this is my father-in-law Bob Cooley."

Firm hand shakes, Bob slapped Claude on the shoulder. "So you're the guy that stole my little girl?"

A big smile let Claude know Bob was alright with it.

He wanted Clara's happiness.

They departed in the wagon. Clara joked, "Had any flats lately?"

Claude cut his eyes toward her. She simply shrugged her shoulders and protruded her lower lip, was it a muse?

They arrived at the DeMoss home, a two-story traditional, white with black shutters. Any woman could tell a man lived there, totally devoid of a woman's touch. No plants, no knick-knacks, not even a welcome mat. The yard was mowed today, the grass clippings were fresh, not raked. Just hurriedly kicked about by the foot.

Inside Danny and Modeena stood at the ready. Claude introduced them to Clara.

Modeena looked from the bottom of Clara's expensive shoes to the top of her head, then did so again.

"So you is da one been keep'n Mr. Claude up all night? I show see why. You gorgeous!" A smile only Modeena could smile welcomed her.

Danny cautiously smiled, shook hands and said, "Welcome to Elmbrook."

Clara smiled back, Danny melted, Clara had already won him over.

At supper Modeena served pork chops, turnip greens mixed with cabbage, new potatoes, corn bread and iced tea. Everyone talked, laughed, even Claude ate a full plate.

After dinner Modeena started to clear the table, Clara started to help. Modeena stopped her. "Honey chil', I see I'm gonna like you. You go visit with Mr. Claude. He been missin' you somethin' awful."

Clara followed Modeena's instructions. She and Claude talked awhile. Claude felt the urge to tell Clara everything, then thought, "No, I can't risk it."

Modeena came by a short while later, her brown grocery sack in hand. "I'll see you in the mornin' Mr. Claude" and winked at him when Clara momentarily gazed away. Claude knew damn well Modeena stayed every night but Saturday, it was Friday.

"Good night, Modeena," Claude said.

Modeena wobbled out the front door, humming some low blues melody. It was a happy tune for her.

"What's in Modeena's brown sack?" Clara asked.

"Well, we don't know exactly tonight. If I was guessing I would say a left over pork chop, what's left of the greens, cabbage, potatoes, and corn bread. Two mason jars filled with fresh tap water and her Salem cigarettes. Maybe a banana or an apple," Claude replied.

"But she ate at the table with us. Does she eat all that?" Clara asked.

"Hard to say. I never go over there. I've been there twice before when she was down with pneumonia. I doubt she eats it, my God, she eats enough here. When Modeena bakes cookies, she and Danny do a lot of test-tasting. I'm lucky to get one or two," Claude replied.

"Where does she go?"

"One block down, across the switching yard tracks. She has a shack that backs up to the tracks," Claude answered.

"Let's follow her."

Claude's back straightened, his head cocked to the side like an inquisitive puppy.

"Why?" Claude said.

"Aren't you the least bit curious?"

"No," Claude replied.

Clara got up from the couch, "Come on, come on."

Hesitantly Claude followed.

It wasn't hard to catch up to Modeena's no hurry walk.

They stayed back far enough to watch. Modeena crossed the tracks, stopped by a switch arm, and rummaged through her sack. Another smaller sack was born. Modeena placed it on the ground and ambled on.

When she disappeared, they approached. Inside the sack were left-overs, each placed in a sandwich bag to keep them separated. At the very bottom was a neatly folded note, scrawled in print:

STAY AWAY FROM MR. CLAUDE.

"What's that about?" Clara asked.

Claude carefully re-packed the sack as it was. Wheels were spinning in his head. He didn't answer Clara for a long, unintentional pause. "Don't know," he finally said.

They returned across the tracks, and hid behind a boxcar. They waited as sundown began.

Clara could sense something had upset Claude. As they were hiding Clara began questioning, "What's this about? Are you in danger? You haven't been yourself in awhile? Is everything OK?"

Intermittent stormy questions delivered in rapid fire fashion. Not enough time between questions to develop an answer. No time to decide to answer. The notebook, the themes.

Claude rolled each question carefully. It was too much to think about at one time. Claude was absolutely silent. Just as Clara was to begin round two of questions, two figures appeared.

They walked to the sack and sat down. They began to eat with plastic forks. Claude thought, Modeena would not put our silverware in that sack, she guards it like its real silver." They brought those forks, they've done this before." The younger of the two came up with the note, handed it to the other. He read it, stroked the stubble of his unshaven face, quietly got up, placing the note in the band of his sweat pants.

Clara let out a short gasp, "Cliff?"

CHAPTER SIX

Modeena showed up right on time as usual to fix Saturday morning breakfast. Claude and Clara were waiting at the kitchen table.

Claude spoke first, "Modeena, how do you know the men who picked up your sack at the tracks?"

A biting look came across Modeena's face. Childish, lost.

"Well, Mr. Claude, they come to da back doe about three weeks ago. Dey's looking all around, askin' all kinds of thangs bout you. I didn't tell dem nuffin'. Jest give 'em some food. Den dey's gets ta follin' me. I got scared Mr. Claude, so I start takin' em food so dey says away from here."

Claude and Clara, both said, "okay" at the same time. Then went outside to talk.

During the night Clara told Claude all about Cliff. How it was a terrible mistake. How lonesome she got when Taylor went away. How much she needed someone after his crash. There was no love, never was. Just someone to fill the emptiness.

Long into the night Claude listened. Clara told him how much she loved him, not Cliff or any other man. Just him. She cried, confessing her deepest fears and sins.

How Marie had subconsciously substituted her for Taylor. Marie spoiled her with expensive, lavish things, but that didn't matter. What she really wanted was a man that made her feel the way Claude made her feel.

Claude's unproven thoughts passed away. They were under

control now. He was convinced of Clara's love, scarce, never-ending love.

With love must come trust, respect. He must trust his secret with Clara.

Claude told Clara the whole story. The   flat, where the drugs were, New Orleans, the white van, the sleepless nights, always looking over his shoulder. How he wanted to go to the authorities but was afraid they wouldn't believe him. It was a wild story. What if they arrested him? Possession was possession.

Clara agreed it was too risky to take the chance of arrest.

Clara knew something Claude didn't. Marie had not become one of the wealthiest women in the south by accident. She had long since invested her money in stocks, bonds, New York real estate, in fact, had aspirations for Taylor to run for Congress.

Influential, powerful people were behind her. Marie controlled everything indirectly in and around Mobile, including the police. If she wanted something done, legal or otherwise she knew who to call.

Claude and Clara's weekend ended. Monday Clara went to see Marie, she told Marie everything, Cliff, Claude, tires and all.

Marie had started the day with a pitcher of Bloody Marys. Clara drank two to bolster herself. Marie drew hard on the Virginia Slim cigarette, took another sip of her drink and began to exclaim.

"I know about Cliff. I have known all along. I know about Claude. I have known all along. I know about the tires. I know about the content of the tires. I know who planted it there. I know who it belongs to."

Clara placed her hand over her mouth, as if to keep from screaming. "Let's bring this to an end. Is there anything you don't know?:

"Yeah, what do you see in Claude?"

"I love him."

"What a laugh, love. Grow up kid. Two things run this world, money and power. You can't have one without the other. I've given you both and you want to trade that for a life in Elmbrook, Mississippi? Get smart! Wake up!"

"What right did you have to spy on me?"

"When I pay all the bills and keep you at the center of my plans. That's what right I have! Your sitting here because I planned to have you here. <u>This day!</u> In your perceived dilemma!"

Marie smiled a chicken shit smirk. "Why, what do you want?" Clara asked trepidly.

Another drag, another sip, a moaning breath of sorts." I was a war bride just like you. A pretty face and figure to match. Absolutely broke. I 'm who I am because of intricate long term planning. You, my dear, have no plans. No, no, You're gonna be right here in Mobile with me. You see Cliff is working off a little debt. We know exactly where the drugs are and we wouldn't want the police to find them would we?"

"Are you blackmailing me?"

"Call it what you will?"

"Why? What do you want?"

"I want <u>you</u>, Here in Mobile!"

"For what, to babysit a pathetic old drunk?"

Marie arched her eyebrows. "Be here in the morning. We have work to do."

Clara stormed out. "I won't be back. I won't."

CHAPTER SEVEN

Clara returned to Marie's the next morning, knowing she would start calling insistently. She had thought about calling Claude, but knew now she was under surveillance. She didn't see anyone follow her. She wondered if her phone was tapped. A police cruiser passed in front of her. Next block another.

Marie's eyes were puffy and bloodshot; the Bloody Marys'were poured. Marie handed Clara a document, it was Marie's will.

Without a word, Clara read.

"So you're leaving me 80% of your estate and Bob, your husband of thirty-five years, 20%?"

"That's right."

"Does Bob know about this?"

"Yes, he's lucky to get that and he knows it!"

Apparently Marie had something on Bob. Bob still loved her even though she had grown mean and bitter. The alcohol didn't help.

"What's the catch?"

"You stay here in Mobile until I die."

"And what about Claude?"

"No Claude, no Elmbrook."

"Why Marie, don't you want to see me happy?"

"Yes, yes I do. But not at my expense. I love you, you're all I have left."

"What will happen to Claude?"

"Nothing if he doesn't do anything stupid."

"Like what?"

"Try to sell the drugs."

"Can I talk to him, explain things?"

"No, that wouldn't be wise."

CHAPTER EIGHT

Clara returned to her waterfront loft. Noticed the door was ajar, a break-in? No, someone was sending her a message. They wanted to let her know she was being watched. Did they bug the place? Tap the phone? Suddenly she felt like a prisoner in her own home. She knew something was up, police cruisers cris-crossed in front and behind her on her way across town. They didn't stop her or even look her way. Their mere presence sent a chill through her, if they had orders to do this, what else were they capable of—murder?

Clara had thought of calling Claude despite Marie's warnings. The phone rang. It was Claude.

"I can't talk right now," she said quickly.

"Okay, I'll call back later."

"No, no, I'll contact you."

She hung up the phone. The receiver met the cradle. Another call.

"Hello." No response. Was Claude calling again or another message? You're covered, that was the message.

Clara went about her business, trying to ignore the surveillance. It got tedious and bothersome, reluctantly accepted. Anytime a friend called, it was followed by another call, the hang up call.

Weeks passed.

She needed to talk to Claude.

Clara went to a payphone and called at 7 PM. She knew Claude would be there.

"Always a busy signal."

A police cruiser always passed as she was trying to place the call.

Marie owned Mobile and the police department.

Clara was captive.

A letter arrived from Claude, it had been opened. So someone knew the contents of the letter. Claude asked to meet her. He would come to Mobile. All he knew was she lived at the waterfront in a loft apartment.

Weeks passed.

3:00 AM Clara was awakened by her doorbell. Someone was standing on it. Pushing it repeatedly, in a panic. She stumbled to the window and peeked out. Claude.

She hurriedly wrote a quick note. "DON'T SELL DRUGS!"

She opened the door and handed him the note. They embraced. When Clara's mouth was close to Claude's ear she whispered, "I'm being watched."

"Let's get out of here," Claude said.

"Let me get my shoes." Clara, already dressed in sweat pants and a t-shirt, hurriedly left with Claude. They reached Claude's station wagon, got in, and pulled away. A police cruiser was on their tail. No lights, no siren, just following along. He had come out of nowhere.

"Take me back. They know I'm with you. Marie will be furious."

"No. So what, we are not breaking any laws."

"That doesn't matter in Mobile. Claude, I'm scared."

They drove toward the Mississippi line, the police on their tail.

They neared the city limits, the cop flipped his lights and siren on, passing them at high speed. Clara and Claude passed the city limit sign. The cruiser pulled to the right shoulder in front of them, punched it and slid across the road facing them. He headed in the opposite direction back into town.

Clara clutched Claude's arm so tightly it was cutting off his circulation, he could feel the fear telegraphing though her.

"See, I told you!"

"Maybe he was just on patrol and got an emergency call."

"No, there was no emergency."

Not far out of Mobile an Alabama State Trooper dropped in behind them. He followed them to the state line. Shortly after crossing, a Mississippi State Trooper appeared.

"Do you think they know about the drugs?" Claude asked.

"No, I don't think so. I think Marie is much more powerful than I realized."

"Claude, she's obsessed with me! She's forcing me to stay in Mobile. She owns the authorities."

"That's ridiculous, this is America, you have constitutional rights. We'll get a lawyer and put a stop to this."

"No, I can't. I can't break her heart. She needs me to survive."

"I need you too."

"I told her I would stay in Mobile."

"Why?"

Clara told Claude everything, everything except the will, oh yeah, the will.

CHAPTER NINE

Claude and Clara arrived in Elmbrook at 9 o'clock. Modeena had walked Danny to school and was busy with the laundry.

Claude asked Modeena to do some grocery shopping. Modeena placed her hands on her hips, buried her chin into her throat, saying," Mr. Claude, you knows Tuesday's is double stamp day." Modeena had decorated her entire shack with articles from the Green Stamp catalog.

"You twos just wants to be together. I ain't no chil' Mr. Claude."

Without mincing any words Modeena proceeded out the door, bound for her shack.

"Are you as exhausted as I am?" Claude asked.

The frailty and helplessness of Clara was visible.

"Yes, worn out, physically and mentally spent."

They climbed the stairs toward the bedroom.

"Do you see what I mean by being captive?"

"Yeah. I'm surprised Marie is that controlling. Are you sure she's behind it or am I about to be arrested?"

"Yes, I'm sure it's Marie" she muttered. Thinking silently if she should tell Claude about the will. It was no longer blackmail, it was an agreement. A deal Clara wanted out of, the money didn't matter. She wanted her freedom, happiness, a life with a man she loves.

Claude moved closer, cupped her face in his hands, and kissed her softly. Suddenly nothing else mattered, they were alone. They slowly undressed each other, their eyes meeting, it was as intensifying as the first time.

Claude slowly lowered her to the bed. The room seemed hazy in the mid-morning light, Clara's head on his chest. "Just hold me." He held her, the fragrance of her hair filled his mind, gently stroking her head and hair as it passed through his fingertips.

Time temporarily vanished. For the first time in a long time Claude felt needed, powerful, strong. Whether Clara knew it or not she was calling for him to claim her.

They fell asleep, exhausted.

CHAPTER TEN

Clara's eyes cracked open slightly, the mid-afternoon sun had awoken her from a deep restful sleep. She was still in Claude's arms. She felt whole, complete.

The transparent white linen curtain was fluttering randomly up and down in the soft spring breeze. She could see a washed red barn in the distance and then a sea of black plowed fields beyond. She tried to picture herself here, what would her life be like? She could help Claude at the compress, spruce up the house, add the touch of a womanly eye. The hardwood floors were worn with an almost dirty look, she had seen a spot or two where old furniture or objects of some kind had been moved, there it was beautiful, a glossy fine-grain wood. Probably pine or oak, she thought.

Claude stirred, rolled over covering her. He began to kiss and caress her neck. She wanted him, his holding her and playing with her had definitely pushed some buttons. It was extended foreplay, the long period of time she had not seen him or the combination of the two, but she was ready. She could feel the tips rising erect beneath her t-shirt, her juices were flowing.

They began to make love, very slowly at first, then Claude would lie perfectly still, composing himself, making certain he did not rush. His touch slow, smooth, light. She could feel the blood rush to the top of her skin. Her face was blush red. The climax, trembling, shuddering, the apex of her sexuality was now. Clara wanted to scream only to intermittently spasmodically jerk. It was by far the most erotic, satisfying event she had ever experienced.

They were perfectly still for minutes. She felt and thought she heard faint little popping sounds coming from somewhere within her. Life was perfect in that peculiarly brief window of timelessness.

CHAPTER ELEVEN

Later that evening after dinner

"We have to do something, this is not working for either of us. I'm miserable with you in Mobile. You're miserable being there. I don't get it, tell Marie your leaving and that's that, over with, done!"

"I've told you Claude. It's not that simple, everything is not black and white, grey abounds in my life, it always has."

"Explain it."

"I don't know if I can."

"Give it a try. Do I have to pull everything out of you?"

"Okay, I love Marie. She's been like a mother to me. I was raised by grandmother, my mother got pregnant when she was fifteen, she had me and left when she was eighteen. I don't blame her. I resented it as a child, but when I turned fifteen myself I realized she was just a child herself when I was born. I bonded with my grandmother, she fed and clothed me, kissed and hugged me, cried when I cried, hurt when I hurt. She was everything to me."

"Where is she now?"

"She passed away a year after I married."

"Who is your Dad?"

"I don't know, I'm not sure my Mom does."

"Where is your Mother now?"

"Last I heard she was working in a bar in Houston. She's never been a part of my life."

"Does your mother have a name?"

"Bobbie, Bobbie Menard. My grandmother's name was Grace Menard. Nan. My maiden name was Clara Menard."

"Would you recognize your mother if you saw her?"

"Of course. I've seen her on and off through the years. She's really a very nice person. I love my mother. We both know now that I've grown up how things were."

"Okay, okay, back to Marie. Why this death grip on you?"

"Taylor was her life blood, he actually gave purpose and fulfillment to her life. Joy, everything important in life is about joy. Think of the people and things you enjoy most and imagine them gone. It's total emptiness. It's the reason people kill themselves."

"So you think Marie may kill herself?"

"Maybe, I don't know. She's doing it anyway the way she drinks. She drinks because she grieves. Taylor was everything to her, her only true joy. She could just not accept the loss. Now I'm her only joy. Don't you get it? I'm Taylor's double."

"Oh shit, I thought you wanted out?" Claude quipped.

"I do. I can't carry that kind of guilt. It's just not right. She loves me in her own way. Doesn't everybody love in their own way? When someone says they love you it doesn't mean shit, that's only telling yourself how you feel inside, it's all about you. When you really love someone it's what you do that counts."

"I thought maybe you didn't want to give up the things she favors you with, the money she forks out and all."

"I grew up on Nan's social security check in a small two bedroom frame. I can't say I don't like having money. That's a joy of sorts, but it's not what I'm about. The things I want are here with you. A home, a family, love."

"Are you being completely honest with me?"

"No, there's more, there's a will."

Chapter Twelve

"So Marie is holding you hostage with the promise of a bequeathment in her will?"

"Yes, there's more. The drugs, Marie had them planted."

"Why?"

"Leverage, blackmail, ace card, call it what you will. She's not going to let me go."

"What do you think she'll do?"

"Since I left Mobile, she will play that card. The local authorities know where the drugs are hidden. You could be arrested any minute."

"How do you know this?"

"Marie told me. She controls and manipulates everything. Believe me, I've learned, she's the queen of dirty dealings."

"You mean all along you've known. I've been suckered?"

"No! I'm trying to put this together. I didn't know how far Marie would take this. Marie gets what she wants, she always has."

"We need to get the drugs and destroy them Clara."

"No, Marie would just plant some more. How do we know there's not more here, in the house, the garage?"

Claude sat on the side of the bed, buried his face in both hands, "My son, Modeena, we're all in danger!"

Clara sat beside him putting her arm around him. "There's only one answer. I have to go back to Mobile."

"No, I've already lost one good woman in my lifetime. I'm not letting it happen again!"

"What can we do?"

There was a deaf silence.

Chapter Thirteen

"Artie Mae"'s here Modeena" Danny said.

"We goin' to da r'ival at da Gospel of the Lord church, Mr. Claude, I'll pray for all you likes I always do. I'll be a prayin' a special prayer for you and Miss Clara, yes sir, a very special prayer" Modeena said with a broad, glimmering smile.

She winked at Danny as she and Artie Mae ambled down the front walk in their finest outfits, complimented with a garb of costume jewelry and outrageous smelling perfume.

Claude and Clara knew Modeena's prayer, she had hinted at it most everyday for over a week. Matrimony was on her mind, she couldn't say, "Mr. Claude, you sho' is lookin' happy today", enough. It had gotten to be a running joke, bringing smiles and giggling to everyone.

Clara had devised a plan. Claude agreed. They would leave the secret beneath the compress floor where it was for the time being. Clara would return to Mobile and appeal to Marie for mercy. She could take her out of the will. The money was not important, she could live without it.

Danny ran across the room and jumped on the couch beside Clara. He was reading his homework assignment to her, The Red Badge of Courage. Clara was extremely patient with him, the two had grown close in the last week. Clara had won him over slowly, not pressing him. It had worked wonders for both of them. Danny's schoolboy crush confirmed his affinity for her.

Next morning Claude and Clara left for Mobile. They were shadowed by the police all the way to Marie's estate. The pair nervously rang the bell, although Clara had her own key. They were let in and joined Marie on the pool patio. Clara was quite sure Marie was on her second or third pitcher of Bloody Mary's.

Clara calmly let Marie know her intentions. The money and the contents of her will didn't matter. She had plans to return to Elmbrook with Claude, today would be spent boxing up her apartment and arranging for a moving van.

Marie was stoic, hardly batting an eye. Somehow in the midst of all the turmoil Marie seemed better. Clara could feel the tumulsion within her, but wasn't backing down an inch. Claude was merely a sideline observer. Marie acted as if he didn't exist.

They left and headed to the loft, unwanted police escort and all, nothing had changed, at least not yet.

The afternoon was spent packing boxes, calling the moving van company. Claude loaded most of the smaller things in his station wagon. Clara's Mercedes was parked where she had left it last week. It had been a birthday gift and was registered in her name. She intended to take it.

Claude left around 6:00 PM in the wagon, Clara was to supervise the moving people and join Claude tomorrow.

Claude got home around 10:00 PM, left Clara's stuff in the wagon and went inside. Clara should be here by six or seven tomorrow, if our plan works. Claude thought, those damn cops were getting on his nerves. I've never so much as stolen a pack of gum. I'm a good man. I don't deserve this shit. It was a nightly re-run. I can't believe the cops are this corrupt, I can't believe one person could have this much control, misused power. It was sickening, the worst part is how quickly Claude was getting used to it.

Claude fell asleep and began to dream. 1963 Kennedy assassination, Lee Harvey Oswald, patsy, gunned down in the Dallas Police Station. Dallas Times Herald head lines. Jack Ruby shooting at point blank range. It looked like a sports freeze-framed photo.

Jack Kennedy's blood pouring from his head. A squad car "to protect and serve."

Claude awoke, his dream too disturbing. He could feel his pulse racing in his neck. Of course the police are dirty. Power, control, authority totally abused.

He knew from this day forward his one time favorable opinion of the police had been changed forever. No, he would change that opinion, they were scum completely capable of murder, frame-ups, any horrific act imaginable.

Clara's red Mercedes pulled up at 7:30 PM. It seemed like she had been gone longer than one night and day. Claude had been waiting on the porch swing.

"Did you get to a phone?"

"Yes."

"Can they help us?"

"They said they can."

"Do you trust them?"

"Not sure, we're really going out on a limb if it doesn't work."

"Do we have a meeting?"

"They said they would contact us."

All their discussions took place outside in the yard. The house was bugged, the phones at home and work were tapped. Everyday life was exhausting.

8 AM Claude stopped to get gas on the way to work. Charlie the attendant started pumping the gas, "You want to fill this 'Big Boy' up Claude?" Charlie? He's filled this car up for seven years. He has always said, "Fill 'er up?" 'Big Boy' is what Clara referred to as Claude's play thing. The hair stood on Claude's neck. He could punch him out, right now. What and have the police arrest him? Claude waited, paid, and drove away.

They know every word being said in my home, including my bedroom. The cock sucking bastards, the goddamn cock suckers!

Claude went to the compress office, tried to do some work, he couldn't concentrate. His mind was too messed up with doubts and fears about the police, Marie, even the goddam gas station attendant. His life was turned upside down, he was determined to get it back. He loved Clara, no one was going to stop him.

Claude strolled back in the warehouse. His long-time bookkeeper, Ortha Joe had gone to lunch. The place was empty. He found himself standing over the planks, the hammer marks still visible where he had straightened and re-driven the old nails. New nail heads would have been an indicator. He looked around cautiously in a full circle, deliberately teetering the crowbar under the planks bit by bit and removed the loose dirt. Retrieved the cooler, placed it in the wagon. Got in and drove away.

I could have never sold this stuff, it's Satan's curse on humanity. Every fiber of my being tells me this is wrong. The thought of it being in my car is repulsive. A sudden impulse put him in a scramble to Mobile. It was as if the car had a mind of its own. This is not the plan! He felt an overwhelming urgency to get rid of it, had his mind been on vacation? All this dawdling procrastination was making him sick.

He drove on in his ill-natured state. Three and one-half hours later he was at Marie's house. There was a hostile viscousness in his own voice he didn't recognize. Danger never entered his mind.

"Marie, here's your goddamn shit!"

Claude then threw the cooler across the marbled entry floor. It flew ten feet and slid another ten before crashing into the oak starter step. The newel post vibrated like a guitar string sending out a low rhythmical tone.

Marie, undaunted, with ever present drink in hand, spoke in a calm insolent manner, "My, my have we snapped?"

Marie, self assured, brazen.

Claude, fuming, teeth gnashing, mad.

The showdown was magnificent. The battle raged for over an hour. Attack, counter-attack. Vengeful retribution by Claude.

Calculating strategy by Maire.

The battlefield finally quieted to a quibble. A total absence of reasoning among the two. At last, Claude made a coherent sentence, "Marie, I love Clara. Whatever it takes, no matter how long it takes, we want to be together."

"Love, what do you know about love?"

"I know how I feel about her inside, here in my heart."

"The question is Claude, how does she feel about you?"

"She feels the same, I know it. I see it in her eyes, feel it in her touch. When she says, 'I love you' I know she means it." Claude was now begging.

"Really? How long have you known each other? I've known about your little affair, one weekend a month for six months. That's twelve days isn't it? Oh and last week. Another seven. Let's see Claude, that's nineteen days all together."

"I haven't thought of it that way, and she hasn't either. I'm telling you, we love each other."

"No, no you don't! You just think you do. You were so horny after your eight years of self-inflicted exile that there were probably sheep that looked good to you."

"LOVE" she screamed. "Love is what a person feels inside about another person. When someone says 'I love you' it doesn't mean shit! It's telling yourself how 'you' feel about 'You'. What's important is what are you bringing to the table? It's what you do that counts."

Claude was silent, inquisitive, he wasn't sure where she was going with this.

"Can you provide her with a new Mercedes convertible every year? Can she shop at Neman's in Dallas? Can you provide her with a house like this? You Claude, idiot Claude, could not pay the interest alone on her credit cards!"

Claude eased toward the entry door. His head was down. Somehow he felt defeated.

"Claude, I'm doing you a favor. She would have broken your heart anyway."

One last jab of Marie's boot up his ass.

Claude sat in the wagon, his forehead on the steering wheel. Letting Marie's shrill voice resonate in his head. Deep down he knew she was right.

He thought, "That cut-throat bitch!"

Creeping back to Mississippi, the ever present police on his ass, Claude thought, "I should have kept the dope and sold it. She was right, I have nothing to offer except love."

Claude and Clara were sitting on the porch swing by 7:30 that evening. Recanting what had happened at Marie's.

Clara whispered to Claude, "Have you heard anything from the FBI? They should have contacted us by now."

Clara's head rested gently on Claude's shoulder. It was a picture of a relaxed, satisfying love. Contentment in a storm....a storm about to RAGE.

CHAPTER FOURTEEN

Claude's routine did not vary, except he had changed gas stations. There was a new station where you pumped your own gas. It was a few cents cheaper, but left a lingering smell of gasoline fumes. Claude didn't think it would last. Where would you get oil changes, flat tires fixed? It was a ridiculous concept in Claude's opinion, but it was working, for now.

Claude proceeded toward the new attendant in a tiny glass box. A young man in his early thirties took Claude's money. "Receipt, sir?"

"Yes," Claude said.

The young man handed Claude the receipt. No one else was waiting to pay.

"Read it carefully," the young man said.

Claude's attention peeked. What a strange thing to say.

Claude looked at the receipt closely. There was a hand written note on it in bold black ink that read: "Agent Jeff Myers, FBI. Buy a newspaper." Claude was nearly back to his wagon, he stopped, returned and stated, "Newspaper please Jeff."

"My name is John," the man stated while pointing to a name tag embroidered in a small circle on his shirt.

John turned to some neatly stacked newspapers, took the one on top and handed it to Claude. Claude paid.

Claude went straight to the compress, closed his door and started rummaging through the newspaper. There on the obituary page was a single note written along the top margin.

"Be careful, you're in danger. Give Clara up."

Claude paused a long time. The FBI is dirty too. They're all dirty.

Marie, indeed, knew people in high places.

Claude sat at his desk, the commodity ticker he checked at least every hour, ground out the reports unnoticed. The tape on the machine coiled up on the floor hour after hour. It was nearing 5 o'clock. Claude had sat all day, cast in a spell, mesmerized, thinking. Had his and Clara's plan to get relief from the police pressure backfired? Was "Jeff" an FBI agent? He hadn't produced any ID, why wouldn't he?

Maybe he was an undercover cop? Maybe a private investigator?

The newspaper, was it a veiled threat? Were they going to kill him? Harm his family? What about Clara?

Claude suddenly rebounded to reality, it was 5 o'clock. Claude gathered the tape on the floor, winding it in a tight roll, placed a rubber band around it and stuffed it in his pants pocket. He would check it later.

Modeena had supper on the table at straight up 6 o'clock, she never failed. Modeena, being a member of the family so to speak, served and ate dinner with Claude and Danny. Always had. Clara's extended visit had not changed that.

After the dinner prayer, Modeena, as always, asked Claude, "How is 'da market doin' today?"

Claude kept Modeena informed, although for the life of him, he didn't know why. Small talk more than anything else. Every now and then he would catch her reading his trade journals and various publications related to trading. It was a pondering thought to Claude why Modeena showed an interest. Nevertheless, they had many evenings at dinner and afterward where the market was their sole source of entertainment and conversation.

Clara was quite impressed by Modeena's knowledge saying, "She's certainly not educated, but she's also certainly not dumb or misinformed."

After supper Claude and Clara went to the haven of their porch swing and discussed Claude's curious day. What were they to do? Tomorrow Claude would stop in for another newspaper.

CHAPTER FIFTEEN

What in the world is this? Modeena tugged the roll of ticker tape from Claude's trouser pocket. It was laundry day every day at the De Moss'. Why let it pile up? Just a load or two every morning.

Modeena unrolled the tape and began to decipher its contents. She had seen the ticker tape on rare visits to Mr. Claude's office, knew the vital contents were of monumental significance to De Moss Cotton. However, as close as Modeena had ever gotten to the machine was watching the tape trickle to a heap and slowly coil back on itself. Every so often Claude would caution Modeena, "Careful, that machine is very delicate."

Modeena would kind of tuck her chin making rolls of skin look like stacked rope. Her eyes bugged out revealing much more white in her eyes. "Mr. Claude, dat mushene can't be dat important."

"Yes it is Modeena. It tells us what's happening in Chicago at the Board of Trade every minute of day trading, how much, what price. It's mighty important. Lifeblood to this company."

"Dat so?"

Her daydreaming of office visits ended. Modenna proceeded down the hall stringing the tape out. Her speed was uncanny for a large woman. Intrigued, she began to examine the tape.

Pork bellies, soy beans, currencies from all around the world. Oh yeah, cotton too.

"Good Gaud!"

Modeena's face was lighted with curiosity. She liked the sound of futures. It meant hope, opportunity, excitement.

By the end of the day there were two empty packages of Salem's crumpled by the ashtray. Modeena was happily exhausted, enlightened. She felt she couldn't get to a broker fast enough. After all, she had managed to save $2,000 dollars. This was her chance, her time to shine. Modeena certainly knew the risks. "Don't take all yo' money to da' dice game," she said, talking to herself.

Dice games in her part of town were common, but sometimes deadly. Twenty dollars could make someone stop breathing. It was a brutal world, something Modeena had been exposed to as a child and teenager. Now her sisters talked about and prayed for those poor unlucky souls at church on Sunday night.

It was 4:30 in the afternoon. She was going to wait until tomorrow, but could not stand it. Modeena called Claude's broker Bill McCormick.

"Don't do it, Modeena. Don't take your life savings and put it up for grabs."

"I want 500 on pork bellies. I want 500 on soy beans. I want 500 on crude oil. I want 500 on cotton. I done picked enough of it, and I ain't never owned none of it. I don't even know where I'm gonna put it."

"Modeena, it doesn't work that way! You never own it. They don't ship it to you. You buy a piece of paper, each paper is one contract, one is usually five thousand pounds, one train car full of grain for instance."

"Now you talkin' Mr. Bill. I know all about trains and what's in dem cars."

"Modeena, please, please don't do this. You'll get eaten alive!"

"No, Mr. Bill, this is my money. I earned it, I saved it. And I can spend it any way I want."

"Good Lord Modeena!"....an interminable pause....

"Long or short, Modeena?"

"What you mean Mr. Bill?"

"Long you think the price is going up. Short you think the price is going down."

An elongated silence.

"You mean I can make money if the price goes down? Now how am I gonna do dat?"

"Modeena, when you take a position, you're basically betting the price you buy the contract at, the price on the tape, will go up or down. Short is down, long is up. So, you want one contract, pork bellies at tomorrow's opening price. Long or short?"

"Long" Modeena said.

"Beans?"

"Long."

"Crude?"

"Long."

"Cotton?"

"Short."

"Modeena, you sure you want to short cotton?"

"Yes sir, dat's goin' down."

"Modeena, don't hold me responsible for your losses. Tell me you won't."

"I won't Mr. Bill."

"Okay, here's how to wire me the money."

CHAPTER SIXTEEN

Claude stopped by to get his newspaper. No John, no Jeff. No whoever the hell he was. Claude bought a paper anyway. No messages. There were only two patrol cars in Elmbrook. Claude passed them both four times a day. Twice to and from work and anywhere else he decided to go.

One day Claude stopped at a stop sign with a patrol car behind him. Claude got out, walked to the cops window, "Herman, why are you following me?"

"I'm not, I'm on routine patrol."

Claude was enraged, but tried not to show it.

"So that's how it is, huh?"

"Yeah," the cop looked disgusted and ashamed, he bowed his head, closed his eyes then pinched the bridge of his nose. It was a clear gesture of remorse and shame.

Claude slammed his car door and drove off.

Now he knew. These guys didn't want to do this anymore than Claude wanted it done. It all went back to Marie. "That black-hearted, shameless bitch!" She had been ruthless in her pressure and pursuit to get Clara back to Mobile.

Claude's fuse was getting shorter. Cotton prices were down. He held enough contracts to cover his inventory. Most of the cotton bales had been shipped to the mills in North Carolina. It had not been a good year. Everything he bought seemed to be going up, the news called it 'inflation'. Maybe he would break even.

The war was finally over. It seemed so senseless. No purpose.

Or maybe there was a purpose, during the war there was little if any 'inflation'. Cotton prices were down, demand from the military for cotton products was up. Hell the war had been good for the economy. Maybe that was its sole purpose, many got downright rich.

Claude thought that would be sad if all these young men, boys drafted at eighteen years of age, some still seniors in high school, were expendable, pawns. A commodity of useful bodies with an indelible stamp on their foreheads: For Government Use Only.

It was a sickening thought. Kennedy in 1963 said we would not enter that conflict. Maybe he was the first to get his head blown off.

Claude, along with a lot of other people, didn't believe Oswald was the shooter. Did it really matter who actually did it? The most alarming and scary thing was who ordered it? Was the fox watching the hen house? They seem to be right now.

"Damn right. It's corruption personified."

"That's my problem, corruption in the bowels of the South. Controlling my life, my destiny. Something has to be done!" Claude was speaking aloud even though he was alone. The stress was building.

"I don't want to be like them. I'm a god-fearing good Christian. A good man, father, employer, person in general." Claude's self-talk seemed convincing. Shit in ice cream, Claude had once heard if a fresh stinking turd is dropped in a big ole tub of vanilla ice cream, it didn't hurt the turd at all, but it sure ruined the ice cream.

"I'm the vanilla ice cream. They're the turds!"

CHAPTER SEVENTEEN

Clara was getting along fine in the two story frame. She had planted flowers and shrubbery, painted the front door a deep burgundy red, really sprucing the place up. The house was being transformed into a creative eclectic cottage style place.

It felt like and looked like a home, the place was okay before, but it lacked that little something extra. A four foot long plank Clara had found in the garage and painted the same deep burgundy red adorned a wall. The calligraphy type white lettering read "Bless this home with love and laughter." The sign described the place, it was much more than a decoration. Here, here in this house that was happening and oh, what a blessing from God it was. The emptiness and sadness of earlier years long past. It was within itself an amazing revelation. Love and laughter.

Clara got a kick out of Modeena's interest in the market. Admittedly she did harbor some pessimism , she knew first hand all about margin calls, unaccountable almost mystic market swings. She was growing to like and respect Modeena even more. She did not want to see her hurt. Financially or otherwise.

Many fortunes have been gained and lost almost overnight. Modeena stopped to think about the day McCormick had asked about her life savings. How she had treaded to the out house and reached through the hole where she usually sat and felt "up under dare" for the fruit jar, its lid ingeniously fastened with a screw from the top through the wood planks and into the jar lid. Modeena's bank was convenient, when she got a rare extra dollar she merely gave the glass fruit jar hanging from the lid a twist and more often than not she left two deposits, one in cash, the other in a more bodily form. Modeena thought that was funny.

She knew wiring him the money was the right thing to do. Western Union office came to mind, how she had gathered all those dirty, crumpled up dollar bills. Those hard earned dollars, she could feel the sweat on them, the blood oozing from her raw, sore, cotton patch hands. Just looking at some of the tightly balled up dollars lying on her bed brought back the pain. The heat, the torturous weight of the sack full of cotton she was dragging along. The anxious always disappointing weight of the cotton before it was dumped in a trailer, just so she could start all over again. The agony and hopelessness that had been her childhood.

She was alone now thinking all those thoughts, a flashback to hell. She could see herself standing over her lumpy single bed with every dollar she had ever managed to save before her. Tears streamed down her face, the pain was too much not to.

How she had counted it out to the Western Union lady, hanging on each dollar as a memory of endless rows of cotton, the sharp stinging pricks of cotton burrs.

 Fact was, Modeena was amassing quite a bankroll. Her initial two thousand was now almost one hundred thousand dollars. She had not shared her new found wealth with anyone. There were subtle, perhaps subconscious, gestures through. The two dollar bills she placed without fail in the church offering were now two crisp one hundred dollar bills. Neatly slipped into a plain "no name" envelope.

Modeena was thankful. Truly thankful to the Lord.

CHAPTER EIGHTEEN

One year later....

Circumstances had remained the same. Claude bought a handgun, he wasn't really afraid, but wanted the comfort of knowing he could protect himself, his family, if need arose.

Clara called Marie after not hearing anything from her for six months. She feared Marie never really loved her, that Marie considered her just another possession. Someone she could control, make jump through hoops for the right price.

Clara was wrong. Marie was devastated, heartbroken, drinking constantly. When Clara called all Marie said was "when are you coming home?"

Clara told her how happy she was, asked her if she wanted the Mercedes back. Marie did not answer her, but she didn't hang up.

Clara talked about ten minutes, telling Marie of her new found home and family. Modeena was teaching her to sew, about the house, Danny, Claude, church, her vegetable garden.

She ended with "I love you and pray for you each night, and I've just found out today I am going to have a baby."

Marie never responded. Clara wondered, did she hear? Had she simply put the phone down or maybe she was so drunk she's passed out.

Clara's pregnancy was coming along six months now, only three more to go.

The day after she told Claude she was pregnant they went to

Memphis and got married. Clara was a beautiful bride, she held no questions in her mind of second thoughts. She knew her lifetime would be spent loving Claude and him loving her.

The baby kicked. Danny was sitting next to Clara on the couch reading to her. The flinch startled both of them. Clara took Danny's hand "Feel here, that's a foot."`

"How do you know that," Danny asked.

"You just do."

Clara ardent, sitting perfectly still. Suddenly out of nowhere tears began to flow. She had an overwhelming urge to call Marie.

The phone rang and rang. She was about to give up when Marie answered, "Hello."

"I was just sitting here thinking of you. The baby is kicking, my hormones are going crazy, I want you here," Clara started to cry.

"Sweetheart, I'll be there tomorrow."

CHAPTER NINETEEN

Bob flew Marie up. Clara was at the airport waiting in the Mercedes. When they hugged, Clara noticed Marie was sober.

"Do you know how long I've waited for a grandchild?"

"Oh no, this is not your grandchild. This is not Taylor's, it's mine and Claude's. Let's get that straight from the start."

"Okay, okay. Will I be able to see the baby?"

"Of course you will, provided you are sober and you don't spoil it rotten."

Marie seemed out of character for a change she was willing to compromise. Clara couldn't help but think she has something up her sleeve. For now she would give her the benefit of the doubt.

It was a beautiful mid May day. The sun was shining, a mild 75 degrees with just a hint of a breeze. The top down on the mercedes made you want to drink the fresh clean air. It was a wonderful feeling. The two rode along chatting.

"How's Bob?"

"Great. We had a little split, but he's back. He had to fly on up to Memphis, something about inspecting the plane's engines. He'll pick me up at five o'clock. That gives us all day. He's anxious to see you, he misses you too."

"How about calling the dogs off?"

"What do you mean?"

"The pressure Marie, the pressure. Don't play dumb."

"I don't know what you're talking about.'

Clara rolled her eyes, thinking I'm not fighting with her today. It's been too long. Time to mend fences. She'll let up when she's ready. I know Marie.

"Maternity clothes, come back to Mobile with me and I'll load you up. We can shop all day."

"No Marie. I make all my clothes now."

"You're kidding? You sew? Where the hell did you pick that up or is that all there is to do in Hickville?"

Clara gave a little smirk, thinking, that's the Marie I know.

Soon they arrived at the house. Modeena welcomed them, Modeena style. Big broad smile, apple pie cooling on the kitchen table. The aroma alone smelled delicious as it permeated throughout the house. This was an all out blitz. Modeena knew Clara's feelings, she was hell bound to make it go good. In typical Marie fashion she walked right past Modeena as if she were invisible. Modeena's brow crinkled, dislike coursed through her. Her chin tucked, eyes looking over vanishing reading glasses. Modeena held her tongue, played the maid role. Modeena thought does this old bitch know what I'm worth?

"Sorry, I can't offer you anything to drink. How about some apple pie?"

"Oh no, I'm watching the waist line."

Clara almost chuckled, but managed to hold it. Marie didn't give a damn about her waist line, health in general. The alcoholic midriff bulge was prominent, along with the leathery lines coursing her face. Marie lite a cigarette, blowing the smoke toward the ceiling.

"Let's get down to business. Claude had two bad years. He doesn't have the capital for another year. The bank won't loan him money. I'll see to that."

"Claude's had bad years before. He's not worried, the banks seen him through bad times before. He's confident they will again."

"No, not going to happen Dear. I bought the bank."

"You what?"

"Be sensible. You come back to Mobile with me and I'll see Claude gets another year."

"I'm six months pregnant and you're trying to blackmail me into coming back to Mobile. That's disgustingly low, even for you!"

"Look kid, I don't know how much time I have left. Sixty two is old, I feel old. When you told me you were pregnant, I suddenly wanted to live again. I will do whatever it takes, you don't want Claude to have anymore tire trouble, do you?"

Clara's back stiffened, cheeks flushed, her jaw was clinched so tight she could feel her molars grinding. "You wouldn't?:

"Yes, I would and I will. Except this time Claude may have to go away for a while...a long while."

It was four thirty. They were sitting in the Mercedes waiting for Bob's plane. They watched silently as he approached, landed, and taxied to a stop.'

Bob ran to Clara, gave her a hug that literally lifted her off her feet. Marie ignored them, taking her seat in the plane.'

"I've missed you girl!"

"Bob you were always one of my favorites. Are you the only one on my side?"

"No, there are others. Once Marie gets her hooks into you, those talons don't drop prey."

"I tried to leave her. She cut me off completely. No plane, no money, I could have lived with that, but she interfered with anything I tried to get started on my own."

"Bob, is there someone else?"

"No, sweetheart, there isn't. I love Marie. But she has become a monster, the bitterness and anger over Taylor's death changed her. She was once a loving person. Her heart and sole was in Taylor, that time was when she was happiest. The three of us spent his lifetime happy, in love, he was our joy."

"I know. He was mine too." Tears filled her eyes, she could see Bob's pain and frustration. Her own mourning.

"Listen Clara, don't come back. No matter what, don't come back. She wants your baby."

CHAPTER TWENTY

Five fifteen Claude's routine did not change. Home right on time every night. Clara was watching for him out the window. Taylor lingered at bars and at the country club, sometimes not coming home at all. Maybe that was why she had strayed with Cliff. It felt like another life.

"I've got to talk to you," Clara said.

"What did she do!" Claude cried.

"She's bought the bank. You won't be able to get a loan for next year," Clara unfolded the days events as they happened.

"She wants the baby."

"I'll kill her, that loathsome bitch!"

"What can we do Claude?" Clara moaned.

"I'm going to kill that....."

Modeena interrupted. "Stop this right now!" making her gravely voice as loud as possible.

Modeena spoke, "I ain't exactly sho what's going on here. All I knows is I ain't never seen the two of you screamin' and a carryin' on like this here! Now who want da the baby?"

"Marie," Clara said.

"I knowed dat woman was no good!:"

"You don't understand," Clara said.

"I understands a heap mo' den you thinks I do. Every maid dats worked for more than a day knows mo' about wants goin' on in a house den the people whats in it!"

"Modeena, please," Clara was unintentionally condescending.

"Modeena, please my ass! I ain't given up da floo. Mr. Claude ain't killin' nobody. Ain't nobody gonna take yoh baby. Dese walls in dis house is mighty thin. Ain't much I don't knows. We in a jam here. First thang we gonna do is pray."

"Dear Lord, Release dis family from the devil's clutches. We pray for our enemies, dat da Lord enter dey life. Cause der Lord if you is in dem they can't be no evil inum. Guide us by yoh light. Deliver us from evil. Direct us. Amen."

Silent as the grave, Claude and Clara knew they had just heard a heartfelt prayer. A prayer that asks for direction, guidance, deliverance from evil. They all knew this was their only choice. They talked way into the night.

Chapter Twenty One

Next morning Claude loaded Clara's Mercedes with her luggage. The goodbyes were especially hard.

They all agreed this would be the only way Claude would get his loan. If he didn't, bankruptcy was close at hand. He only owed five thousand on the house, but if he didn't have a job he didn't have a house in Mississippi.

Clara arrived at noon. Marie had lunch served by the pool.

"You have a new maid," Clara said.

"Yes, they are all new. You can't trust them you know. They'll steal you blind. I change them out every six months or so."

"How clinical, like changing tires."

"Sarcastic banter is not necessary."

An overwhelming urge to get up and run away crossed her mind. She fought it off.

Marie placed three new credit cards on the table. They were in Marie's name, the same as the others were.

"This afternoon, we'll go shopping. Anything your heart desires. Tomorrow we'll get you a new car. What is that one you're driving? Two years old?"

"No, Marie, I'm tired, I need a nap."

Marie seemed put out, but didn't argue.

"Very well, perhaps in the morning."

Clara climbed the stairs up to her old room. The one before she had found the loft. It brought back old memories. Some good, some not. She seemed so distance from this setting. The musty smell of the fabrics, reminded her of a living tomb. She opened a window as if the fresh air would carry away her past. She stood there looking out across the vast estate. The harbor cranes faint outline in the distant horizon.

Clara climbed into bed and began to read, LaMaze Natural Childbirth, she had read it once throughly, but wasn't convinced it would be enough.

"Yes, cover to cover, one more time," whispering to herself.

Marie entered unannounced, not even a knock.

She came straight for Clara, kissing her forehead, gently brushing her hair with her hands.

"We'll have a great time until the baby comes. We need baby clothes, maternity clothes, cribs, car seats...Oh we need a nursery room."

Maire's eyes caught the title of the book on the bed. La Maze Natural Childbirth..

"Oh child, forget that. That's much too risky. You'll have a C-section. That's the way to go. No labor pains. No stress on the baby."

"Marie, I plan to have the baby at home in Mississippi in my own bed!"

"No, by God you won't! That's ridiculous! I will have the very best doctor in New Orleans flown here a week before the due date. That's called a plan Clara, not a seat of the pants, we'll get there somehow bullshit! Successful people make plans, intricate, detailed plans. Why don't you listen to me. Successful people make plans."

"Marie, think what you will! You're not successful, your pathetic! You beg for love. You take what's not yours. Success to you is money, things, even people to you Marie are possessions. Don't you understand Marie, happiness, joy can't be bought. It comes from giving. Giving of yourself, sacrificing your will to the will of God."

"Good. God. Now you've gone off the deep end. Did that nigger maid and hick Claude lead the little sinner to redemption? God, if there is one, would give one the brains to figure things out about the real world. Not fantasy. Do you know where you live?"

"Marie, I swear, I'll get back in that car and go home. You're why

I'm here. How I got to where I am right now. I don't know why God is putting me through this, He must have a reason. But I'll tell you this as long as I'm here I will conduct myself as a Christian. Take your credit cards, gifts, cars and give me my life back!"

CHAPTER TWENTY TWO

Clara called home at 5:20. Modeena answered. Claude was not home yet.

"That's not like Claude. Where is he?"

"Can't say."

"Modeena, I don't know why God is putting me through this."

"Child, God don't put you through nothin'. He's dere to see you through, to give you comfort, to trust in his presence. Satan's in 'dat woman's heart, it's Gods job to get him out. Not yours!"

Clara could hear the tinkling of ice in Marie's glass coming down the hall.

"I'll call back later."

Marie shoved the door open and stood, posed, in the doorway, "Cocktail time."

"Marie, I don't drink anymore. I'm pregnant!"

"Oh, a few won't hurt you. I drank when I carried Taylor."

Marie tripped over her own words, a pale, startled expression. Clara thought, she's remembering. The feeling of being pregnant never leaves a woman. It's a completeness, an innate purposefulness, an inexplicable fullness of life and joy.

A tear was welling in the corner of Marie's eye. She blamed it on the cigarette smoke. Clara could see right through her, she did have a heart.

Clara called home again after dinner.

Claude explained where he had been. Changing tires, no he

didn't buy new ones. Just took the old ones off and checked them out. Clara knew, as all wives do, "what he was thinking."

Clara felt bad for him, he didn't deserve this stress and pressure. The police cover, the phones, the threat of jail for uncommitted crimes. Over a year now, would it ever end?

They talked about Danny, Modeena, the baby, even the garden Clara had planted. Claude promised to look after them. There was a sadness in his voice. "I love you."

"I love you too."

They hated being away from each other, each gave freely whatever they had. Sometimes they would just pass each other and stop, hugging, gently touching, looking into each other's eyes, this was love. They would die before one would let harm befall the other. Both of them knew if this part of their lives ended love was dead. Right now, today, it seemed impossible.

CHAPTER TWENTY THREE

"Why isn't Bob around?"

"He moved to your old loft a few months ago .We were paying for it anyway, hoping you would come to your senses."

"Would he come to dinner here?"

"I'm sure he would, we're still married....but, I think he has found a new life."

Bob showed up right at seven. Marie let the maid let him in. Clara could tell Marie missed him by the dress and jewelry she was wearing. There was a hint of perfume.

Clara met Bob in the entry way. They greeted with a huge hug as usual. Clara whispered, "I think someone misses you." Bob grinned shyly.

Marie turned and there was Bob. He looked into her eyes, the gaze was definitely longer than casual. He hugged her telling her she looked beautiful. Marie couldn't return the hug, a drink in one hand and a cigarette in the other.

"How are the plane engines?" Business before pleasure.

"Both overhauled. It cost five thousand each."

"I'll write them a check."

"Okay, it's your plane."

"How have you been doing?"

Bob actually wanted to know. He had not stopped loving her for a second. He got to a point he couldn't stand to be around her, she had become abusive, yelling, screaming, a form of mental torture designed to drive him away. There were no conversations, only bout after bout of yelling.

Bob knew Marie, really knew her, really loved her.

He did not like her business associates, so called friends, and most of all the dirty politics. The scum of earth camouflaged in black tie affair attire. Most of them were small potatoes feeding off of hardworking blue collar types, stealing their land and houses by misuse of their offices. They had more plans to swindle, than Bob had flight hours. Bob was actually repulsed by the loud mouth no good sons of bitches.

Marie could and would enlist any one of them for her own plots.

"Okay, Bob, how have you been?"

"Good, good."

It was a damn lie. He was more miserable away from her than in the living hell she had created. He didn't understand why? He didn't need to know, he needed to endure. He was another victim. Victims one and two in her parlor having a drink before dinner.

The bell rang again. Bob and Clara looked at each other. Who could the unbeknownst guest be?

"Why Cliff, so nice you could come. You know my wonderful husband Bob, of course you do. And I know you know this sweet little thing, Clara."

Bob looked bewildered. Who was this guy? I don't remember him.

Clara's mouth was open in shock. Totally unforseen, astonishment.

"Double whiskey, straight up, right Cliff?"

"Yes, that'll do for starters Marie."

They drank the drinks and as was the custom had another round and another, and another.

It was 10 PM before dinner was served. The happy hours complete. Clara stuck to a single glass of milk. Cliff and Marie, and Bob could definitely put the booze away. Cliff was actively flirting with Marie. Bob doing his best to ignore it, after all he had 35 years of experience with Marie's shady degradation.

The meal progressed although Marie was not eating, opting for yet another drink. Clara had noticed Cliff's glances, she certainly had looked better, almost seven months pregnant didn't help. Did Marie know about Cliff? Of course she did, she kept tabs on everyone.

Marie was getting drunker, flirting shamelessly with Cliff. He was returning her advances in spades. It was the worst show of rotten to the core behavior a woman could do to a man. The only way it could have been any worse was if it were in public. Bob couldn't take anymore. He slapped his napkin on the table, knocking his chair over, stumbling away from the table.

"I can't take it!"

The front door slammed shut.

Clara's face was stoic, then she began to tremble.

"You cold blooded bitch!"

Cliff and Marie were still laughing.

Clara picked up her dinner plate and threw it in Marie's direction. The drunks attention was finally diverted as it crashed against the wall.

"Cliff, get your ass out of here."

He managed to stand, and ambled to the door.

"Hey, wait a minute," he mumbled.

"Hell no, you son of a bitch, get out!"

Marie could hold more liquor than most men, Cliff was huge and she had just drunk him under the table. She looked amazingly sober.

"What?"

"Marie, you just crushed your husband of 35 years. That was unbearable to watch. Do you have a conscience? You vile, repulsive, sickening piece of shit! You deliberately antagonized and shamed him. You set him up. You brought him here for the kill. The man that loves you! I will never forget this day as long as I live. You are the most dishonorable, unworthy woman God has placed on this earth! You egotistical, vain, conceited demon from hell. May God have mercy on you!"

Clara was running out of words. She knew it was impossible to describe hell. Unendurable, excruciating mental and emotional pain.

At last she left the table, Marie could hear her slamming the bedroom door.

Clara laid across the bed. The baby was still. She was trembling even more, trying to quieten herself. Clara breathed into the pillow. I'm hyperventilated. I need to calm down. Suddenly there was pain, the bed was wet.

CHAPTER TWENTY FOUR

Mobile General Hospital

Claude, Bob, Modeena, and Danny were in the waiting room of the intensive care unit. Thirty nine hours had passed since the dinner party. Two lives at a low ebb. The lines on Clara's monitor were plunging, dipping up and down. One did not need to be a technician to see and hear the erratic flounder. They could go in to see her one at a time for five minutes. Each were waiting their turns.

Claude went first, Clara was unconscious, he held her hand and watched the machine flitter and flicker. There was an uneasiness, what if the beeps and lines on the monitor stopped. Could he bear it? He knew he couldn't.

The next hour Bob went in, he wanted to touch and see her face. It was obscured by tubes, tape and an oxygen mask. Bob held her hand. He talked to her even though he knew she couldn't hear. "We love you, may God be with you."

The next hour Modeena went in. She started talking before she got to the bedside. "My God, My God in heaven. Please Der Jesus don't let nuthin bad happen. Be with her Jesus, stay wiff her. We need boff dese babies back home, back in Mississippi. I knowed she didn't need to be down here in Mobile."

Without warning the machine made a series of quick, faint beeps, paused and a straight flat green line appeared, no beeps. An oversized period mark ran only the line, there were no sounds.

"Oh Lord, Oh Lord!"

Modeena knew something was terribly wrong, People from nowhere appeared, jockeying into well planned positions. Modenna stood back. Someone said, "Get her out of here!"

Modeena some how made it to the hallway. She stood outside the door. Two or three people were running toward her from both directions, they sprang through the door like cats. Modeena felt faint, her head was spinning, nauseous, she went down on one knee, then the other. Modeena was down.

"Modeena, Modeena....Modeena. I'm Dr. Newman. Can you hear me?"

Modeena's eyes fluttered. Her head rose quickly, there was something under her nose. She came to. The lady beside her in a white coat said, "Take this and whiff a smell until things are clearer."

Claude, Bob and Danny flanked her from the sides and front. Her back was against the wall. Legs wide apart, she was beginning to focus on her shoes as she sat on the corridor floor. For some crazy reason she said, "I got dese down at Sears."

Minutes later, two doctors emerged from the room. She's okay. There was apparently a malfunction of the heart monitor. She's not out of the woods yet."

"Can we see her?"

"No, no visitors for at least twenty four hours. She's had enough excitement."

Modeena, still on the floor, "We sho' has!"

CHAPTER TWENTY FIVE

Neo-Natal Unit

"How's the baby?" Marie asked.

"He's very critical. We are trying to stabilize him. Once that's accomplished, gaining weight and growing will be the priority. At 3.9 pounds that will be a while."

"Can't I see him?"

"He can be viewed, but you won't be able to touch him or hold him for now."

Marie hung up the phone, she had not left her house since the ambulance had taken Clara away. Somehow in her distorted concepts, she was not to blame. Accountability for her actions no matter how rotten never seemed to matter. As long as she got what she wanted, who she hurt didn't matter. Marie's only concern was that she came out on top, scot free. Marie always got what she wanted and she wanted the baby.

The next morning sitting at the pool patio table gulping her first pitcher of Bloody Mary's, she was busy plotting her plan of action.

Methodically planning. Get rid of Clara. Not that won't work. I'm not her mother. I have no claim to the baby.

Adoption. Yeah, I could adopt him. No, Claude's the father, he'll get him.

Divorce. Yes, divorce. If she divorces Claude, she'll get custody. The mother always gets custody. Now, how to break them up. That won't be easy. He loves her so much. And that will take some time.

Time is something I don't have. Claude has to die. I could kill the bastard myself for stealing her away in the first place. Cliff was supposed to be the father anyway. I don't know why she didn't get pregnant by him. I switched her birth control pills with placebos. God dammit that should have worked. The little bitch, that was my sole purpose for her. Taylor should have been the father, then I could have rid myself of her. I'm good at that, ridding myself of people. People that I don't need.

Kill Claude.

I've never killed anyone. Oh, yes I have, many times. New Orleans is full of people, expendable people, who will do the job. Remember your first rule: **Always kill the killer**.

That's worked so well throughout the years for me. My own design. I'll get some low life desperate bastard to do Claude. Then I'll call in the pros to dispose of him. No one ever cares about those killings, they don't even make the papers or the news. What would the headlines read?

"Junkie found dead from overdose."

"Single car accident claims life of unemployed man."

"Police shoot man brandishing knife."

"Florida gator found eating corpse."

Marie was growing tired of entertaining herself. This is serious, so much for fun. Claude will die.

CHAPTER TWENTY SIX

Clara's condition was improving, the doctor's say at least one more day in intensive care, then they'll reevaluate her. Claude, Bob, Modeena and Danny had not left her side. Their prayers were working.

Bob hadn't prayed in years. He remembered when he was on flying missions in the war, those prayers worked. Why had he stopped?

The nurse came out. "She's awake."

"You can all see her now, five minutes."

The oxygen mask was gone, only an IV dripping at a snail's pace.

"How are you?" Claude asked.

"How's the baby?" Clara answering with a question.

"He's going to be okay."

"Oh, it's a boy, what does he look like?"

"He looks just like Danny did as a baby."

"That's wonderful. I hoped he would."

"I thought you said you didn't care what it was as long as it was healthy."

"When I looked at the scrapbooks, Danny was a beautiful baby. I wanted a boy, just like him. I love him so much."

Tears were in their eyes. Claude remembering Danny's birth, how amazingly Evelyn's pregnancy had gone full term. How lucky he was then and now.

Clara knew she was blessed. Claude, Bob, Modeena, Danny, and

_____

"What are we going to name him?"

"Well, we've been praying. Bob has been so supportive. His prayers lead me to believe he loves you so very much."

"What do you think of Bob?"

"That would be wonderful."

"Actually, I'm Robert of course, Robert Boone LaSalle."

"Where's Marie?"

No one answered until Bob finally spoke.

"She couldn't make it today."

"Bob said it as if she had been there, everyone but Clara knew better.

"You always cover for her, don't you Bob?"

Clara knew too.

Clara was moved to a regular room. Nurses wheel-chaired her to the neo-nursery. He was so tiny, she called him "Tincy baby."

An overwhelming sense of pure love, tenderness, devotion, came over her. It was a feeling like no other she had ever had. She knew from that moment on he would never leave her heart.

CHAPTER TWENTY SEVEN

"Doctor's say it may be a month or more before he'll be strong enough to be released."

"Go with me today to see them," Bob was calling from the loft.

"Okay, will they let me see the baby?"

"You mean Bob Junior?"

Bob got a big kick out of saying that, the baby's real name was Robert Taylor De Moss.

Marie and Bob were gazing through the plexiglass viewing window. Nurses had rolled his incubator close enough to see him better.

"Look at that blonde hair, would you."

"Oh, he's adorable, isn't he Bob?"

"Don't you think you should show a little more interest in Clara?"

"No. She blames me for this, doesn't she?"

"No Marie, she doesn't. But I do."

"You're going to sober up and turn your life around."

Maire sheepishly peeked around the door frame of Clara's hospital room. The bed was cranked to sitting up, there were remains of the god-awful food on her plate. The dessert she was eating was okay, some kind of pudding. Bob started talking before he got through the door.

"Hi'ya Sweetheart" somewhat of a paraphrase of "Here's Johnny."

"You seem more chipper today."

"Yeah, life is good. There are good people in the world after all."

"And who might that be?"

"Your family, and Modeena."

"Modeena is family ."

"That's what I mean."

Marie had inched herself a few steps into the room. Clara stopped eating and lifted her arms high and apart, beckoning a hug. Marie stiffly complied.

"Well, how have you been?" Marie said.

"Isn't he adorable?" her mind and spirit lifted so, she couldn't think about herself. Clara answered.

"Yes, he is adorable. I like his name: Robert Taylor La Salle. Nice ring to it as long as you don't call him Bob." She drew the name out in a low monotone as if she was saying crap.

"Well Marie, we are going to call him Bob and the last name is De Moss, not La Salle."

Bob smiled, you would think he was the happiest grandpa on earth. Yet he knew there was no blood relationship, but it felt like it. He was savoring the moment.

Marie rolled her eyes.

"Marie, you don't know how lucky you are. Bob loves you and you seem determined to drive him away. Why?"

Clara was being abrupt, challenging. Her voice was growing louder and more rapid.

Bob quickly grabbed Marie's arm and gently pulled her to the hallway. Clara could hear Bob scolding her. "Marie, she doesn't need any of your shit today, for that matter, any day."

Clara smiled as Bob escorted her away.

Claude was coming down the hall, facing them, as they passed.. Bob had the look of a principal taking a belligerent brat to the office.

When they got in the empty elevator Claude released her arm, his knuckles were white.

"I want you to take me to New Orleans today."

Bob knew what that meant. Every time Marie went to New

Orleans something foul was about to happen. Bob knew too much, but never the details. Bob was a good man, caught in a web, with a woman he loved.

"You're going to take that kid away from her aren't you?"

"Why, whatever gave you that idea?"

Bob pushed the down button on the elevator, when it started to descend, all Bob could think about was hell. The doors opened, light and air rushed in from the outside. Bob dropped a dime in a pay phone.

"Get my plane ready, please."

They drove straight to the airport. Pre-flight check, Bob always did it. This time he didn't.

Marie nervously asked, "Why didn't you do your pre-flight check. You always do a pre-flight. You're meticulous."

Bob taxied to the end of the runway. There the planes waited for clearance from the tower to proceed, but today there were no other planes waiting. Bob slammed the throttles full bore. The plane climbed out. They had flown this route many times, about five minutes out Bob should bank a turn along the coast. He didn't, he headed straight out, out to sea.

"Where are you going?" Marie asked in a hushed voice.

"Marie, we have just enough gas to get us about one hundred miles out."

"What? Are you crazy?"stammered Marie.

"Yeah, Marie, I am." Bob flew on.

Marie was shaking, her mouth quivered. She started to beg. "I'll do anything, anything you want!"

Bob, smiled and flew on, an hour, nothing but ocean as far as the eye could see.

Bob reached for the number one engine throttle and feathered it. Then the number two. The plane nosed over. Bob was watching Marie, she wet her pants. The urine was dripping from the seat and into the floor. The twin began to roll, first one time, then another and another. The dive held them tightly against the seats. The G forces disfigured their faces. Urine was suspended in air, slushing about the cabin and onto the windshield. At the last possible moment Bob kicked the rudder and began a hard pull on the yoke. The ocean faced them straight ahead, straight down, in a deep suicide dive. Bob punched both throttles full. Amazingly the plane righted itself and began to rise to level. The waves lapped at the underbelly of the plane as it skimmed the ocean surface. Then Bob began to slowly ascend. They continued south. South toward South America.

CHAPTER TWENTY EIGHT

Ten years Later.

The De Moss' the mail box read: Claude and Clara, Modeena, Danny, Bobby

drawn free-hand in black lettering on the white box.

Modeena reached into the box. The letter was post marked Argentina, return address, Bob.

Claude and Clara read the letter together. They had assumed the plane went down.

Bob Here,

Hope you're all doing well. Marie and I are fine. We have been living in the rain forest of Argentina, actually on the edge of it, accessible only by plane. I have another one now by the way.

Marie has quit drinking. I buy the supplies, booze ain't on the list. We have taken the proceeds of our property and businesses to run an orphanage. There are lots of kids that need our help. They love us and we love them. Marie and I are happy, I think for the first time in our lives.

We wish you well and may God bless you and keep you.
Bob

PART TWO

CHAPTER TWENTY NINE

"My name is Danny De Moss, I'm happy to be here today as the president of the 1972 graduating class of Mississippi State University. May each of you be successful in your chosen fields as you have been here at our alma mater, Mississippi State University."

Danny eased away from the podium, raised his hands high over his head with his diploma in hand saying, "God Bless you all."

Outdoors after the ceremony Claude, Clara, Bobbie, and Modeena stood among the others milling about the crowd seeking their new graduate. Modeena spotted him first. "Mr. Danny, Mr. Danny, we over heara!" Danny ambled up, "Well Dad, I did it." Claude replied, "I never had a doubt." Clara chimed in, "We're so proud of you." Bobbie gave him a slow short right jab to the upper arm, "Way to go."

Modeena always had the right words at the right time, "I'm starvin, lets go get some cheeseburgers. I'm buying." They all gathered at a local joint called Kelly's. It was packed, everyone knew they had the best cheeseburgers around and the beer was ice cold.

Claude and Modeena talked a little business. Modeena had made a fortune trading, so much in fact, she had bought Claude out. The cotton market was shot to hell, the Vietnam war was over.

In the beginning the military bought huge contracts. Nearly every item except wool blankets were made of cotton, from bed sheets to uniforms, it had been an exceptionally good run. Modeena, alert and clever as ever, had made millions. She was among the richest women in Mississippi.

Claude bought his farm although he still lived in town in the same house. He was happy being a farmer, Modeena kept him abreast of the market, "You plant dem soyabeans and stays away from plantin' dat cotton Mr. Claude. No sir, ain't no money in dat, unless you go short on it, you know, like I did befor' the war." Claude knew damn well Modeena was accurate, concise, and clear saying, "Modeena, I've learned never to go against your advice. Just think of all those years I had you doing laundry, if I'd taken you to work I'd be in the Bahamas with you."

"Now Mr. Claude, yo' home is here, mine is too. Dat place down there is my winter house."

Danny broke in on the conversation, "Modeena, are you coming back this summer?"

"Honey chil', I is back, you lookin' at me ain't chu?"

Danny grinned his crooked little Elvis smile, knowing not to push Modeena too much for details of her whereabouts. She had become pretty secretive about a certain male church member and "comins and goins'" as she put it.

Finally Clara got a word in, "Danny, have you decided what to do career wise?"

"Yeah, Mom, you know I'd like to be an airline pilot, but the markets flooded right now with pilots leaving the military. I thought maybe I'd come home and help Dad with the farm."

Modeena jumped in with both feet. "Gaud damn, you done gotz all this schoolin' and you sittin' here tellin' you want to hold a steerin wheel on a tractor? My Gaud boy, whats wrong wiff you."

Danny rolled his eyes, "Modeena."

Bobbie was cracking up at the conversation, he hadn't been exposed to Modeena that much. She had gone out on her own after he turned five.

The cheeseburgers arrived and everybody dug in. Modeena, true to her word, would not let anyone pay, not even the tip.

The parking lot was crowded, people still trying to get in, others wanted out.

Modeena's stretched black Lincoln limousine pulled to the curb in a no parking zone. They all hopped in, Modeena spoke to her driver, "Charles, hurry up. I don't want to pay no ticket." Wasting money was not something Modeena did. She remembered all to well the sting of cotton burrs.

"Charles, take us to da De Moss house."

"Yes 'um" the tall dark, quite handsome driver replied.

He looked very familiar to Claude . He leaned toward Clara and whispered, "Isn't he the church member that Modeena goes on and on about?"

"Yes, yes he is," Clara replied in a hushed voice.

Claude closed his eyes, arched his eyebrows and shook his head gently from side to side.

Danny said, "Modeena do you realize I'm probably the only graduating senior president to be picked up in a limo by their former black maid?"

"Yes, chil', I show do, I show do. Ain't God Great!"

The entourage arrived at the De Moss place. There was a station wagon parked outside, not Claude's old '57 red Plymouth, it was a Chevy two or three years old.

"Now who could that be?" Claude said.

Everyone was clueless, then one by one they began to pile out. Modeena was last, she needed ample room to maneuver. Her feathered hat slightly askew when she finally emerged.

The front door to the De Moss house opened right before they all got to the porch.

A long time, almost five years had passed since Modeena had retrieved the letter from Argentina. It was Marie, at least Clara thought it was. Clara looked closer, "Marie? Marie."

"Yes, it's me."

It was Marie alright. Clara couldn't picture her without a cigarette and drink. Marie always wore tons of make-up and paid particular attention to her hair. Clara had a mental picture of her flitting about the pool patio in one of her colorful, flowery moo moos. This woman had short cropped hair, no make-up, clear eyed, alert and most fascinating a huge broad smile.

"Could this really be Marie?" Clara thought.

"You look different," Clara said.

"Yeah, no frills in the jungle," Marie said.

"Where's Bob?" Clara asked.

"He couldn't make the trip, he's not well, been having some heart problems. He saw a specialist in Miami last year, has to take nitroglycerine tablets."

"Oh, I hate to hear that, why didn't he come with you or at least call?"

"You know Bob, always on the go, besides he had to get back to our orphanage with critical vaccinations and antibiotics. He is a wonderful man, God has blessed me in so many ways."

Clara couldn't help herself, this was too much to take at one time. Did she just hear Marie praise Bob and count her blessings?

"What is she up to?" Clara felt guilty for having the thought. People change, people change she told herself.

"Well come in and sit down."

Each of them passed as Marie stood at the doorway. She smiled, greeted, and hugged each one of them. Even Claude and Modeena. She took a particularly long look at Bobbie, kissing him gently on the cheek and pulling him closer to her.

Bobbie was twelve years old and had never seen or heard of this woman. Who was she he wondered?

They all sat in the living room, Marie began to tell of life in Argentina.

"Well, I'm here, of course, to see you, but I have great need of a new pilot. Bob's been grounded by American standards. He still flies our supplies but both of us know it's only a matter of time before he has a heart spell while flying."

Danny's eyes lit up. "I'm looking for a pilot job."

Marie, courteous for a change, politely told Danny, "This is not an ordinary job. You would be flying over miles and miles of open roughed terrain, then dense impenetrable jungle. It's far too dangerous for an inexperienced pilot, have you ever landed a twin engine plane on a 1000 foot bumpy grass runway?"

"No" Danny said in a disheartened tone.

Everyone was silent momentarily.

"Well," Claude said, "it certainly sounds exciting, but I wouldn't let him do that far all the tea in China."

"Or all the flour in your tires," Marie quipped back.

Claude's face turned flush red. The Old Marie was still under this new found fascade.

Marie continued the conversation with Danny. "Piloting is only a small part of the job, load and unload the plane, teach school and Bible classes, cook, clean, give inoculations, tend to the sick, those sorts of things."

Modeena said, "You been doin' all dat?"

"Yes, I have, I'm proud to say. Oh there's more, every other Sunday we fly a priest in for Sunday morning Mass, fly him back on Monday. It's a short trip by our standards, only 500 km."

"So, doin' the Lord's work?" Modeena said.

"Yes," Marie replied.

Modeena started digging though her oversized handbag. "I gots to where I is by giving to the Lord."

Modeena wrote a check for $200,000. "What's da name of yoh charity?"

"The Orphanage of Divine Mercy."

Modeena scribbled in the name and extended the check to Marie.

Marie glanced at the sum, did a double take, then another.

"What's the catch?" Marie hesitantly replied.

"Find yo self another pilot," Modeena snapped.

CHAPTER THIRTY

Marie stayed for supper. Modeena insisted on cooking, Clara tried to help in spite of Modeena saying two cooks in the kitchen is one too many.

"Boys go upstairs," Clara said entering the living room where Marie was talking with them. Claude had retired early, Marie was not a pleasant surprise. He was glad she hadn't perished at sea, but all the pain and suffering she had inflicted some twelve years ago still hurt him .It had become an underlying deep seated mistrust of everyone. Bottom line, Claude didn't trust her, he knew how vile and vicious she really was, capable of hurting and torturing the innocent, only for the pleasure to watch them writhe in pain for her own self-serving gain. He hoped Modeena had not been duped, what could he do? Modeena did as she pleased, always had.

"Well, Marie, how long will you be staying," Clara said.

"Just today, in fact, I was about to leave."

"Where will you go?"

"Back to Mobile, I still have the house there, it's boarded up."

"Will you go back there someday?"

"No, I'm putting it up for sale, the orphanage needs money. Bob's not going to last forever. I'm putting things in order, my affairs and all. I've changed my will, leaving everything to my cause in Argentina. Do you object?"

"No, not at all. My happiness is here with Claude and my boys," Clara said.

"And my happiness and joy is with my boys and girls, there's so much left to do and so little time. I have to find someone to carry on my work after I'm gone."

"Well, Danny is an ROTC pilot, he barely has 80 hours total flight time in single engine, he's not your man."

"I thought it would be worth a try, Bob would train him in our plane. You know and trust Bob don't you?"

"Yes, Marie, I trust Bob, I just don't want Danny down there, it's all too dangerous. I'm his mother and I want him here."

"Of course you do dear, I understand." Marie stood erect. "I must leave now, may I say goodbye to the boys."

"Of course. Boys."

Danny and Bobbie bounded down the stairs. Marie hugged them and said her goodbyes.

As Marie got in her car Clara leaned inside, "There's something that has always bothered me, was that dope or flour?"

Marie grinned the wickedest look on her face. "I can't give up my trade secrets, now can I?"

The Chevy made a small cloud of dust as it's taillights faded away. Clara walked to the end of the driveway watching the wagon get smaller and smaller until it was gone. She felt differently about Marie somehow, had she turned her life around dramatically with Bob's love and help? Or would she stop at the closest liquor store and transform? Clara let out a heavy sigh, it was good to see her, but it also brought back unpleasant memories. Times long since removed.

It was dusk now, Clara could see lightening bugs blinking in the front yard as she sat on her porch swing. Inside through the window she could see her family and Modeena and Charles. It was a Norman Rockwell of her home, happiness and joy. She said a little prayer to herself, and slowly, very slowly, as if to breathe in as much love and happiness as she could hold, made her way inside.

Danny rose at the crack of dawn. Claude was cooking ham and eggs, the smell of fresh coffee drifted from the doorway of the kitchen and down the hallway to the last few steps of the stairway.

Danny stood there a moment, taking in the fresh brew and smells of home. He took a deep breath through his nostrils, thinking life couldn't get much better. Deep within him was what is in all young men, travel, adventure, a strong inexplicable lust to wander. He felt it for the first time, a strangeness, a feeling of this is Mom and Dad's house, I love it, but its not mine. Where is my destiny? Where will my life take me? Why am I having these thoughts, I'm happy here?

Danny fresh, alert, feeling physically strong and ready to work slid into his appointed chair at the twenty year old dinette set. It was his chair, where he had always sat. That was Mom's chair, Dad's, Bobbie's. At once he felt comfortable, relaxed, then just as quickly he had a pang of something is just not right.

He had been away to college for four years, that was true, there were many times he had come home for the weekend, and always on Thanksgiving and Christmas.

Suddenly Claude interrupted his daydream.

"Grab those buttermilk biscuits out of the oven, I'll burn this gravy if you don't."

Danny quickly retrieved the biscuits saying, "Dad did you ever feel just like you didn't know where to go or what to do?"

"Sure, plenty of times, I was younger of course. You just stay here until you get things straightened out. Stay forever if you like. I want what all Dad's want. I want you to be happy."

Danny and Claude savored their breakfast and coffee. It was time to lay out the day's work, which fields to plow. What should we plant this year, next year? It was a planning strategy table and a lot more. They talked, laughed, told each other off-color jokes before Mom came down. It was their time, a wonderful secure time.

Danny pulled the lift on the tractor, the giant plow rose, the tractor spun 180 degrees. He pushed the lift down, the RPM on the engine grunted down as the plow dug into the rich black earth. Another long monotonous run of freshly turned earth, the smell of the dirt was sweet. Danny liked the smell. Birds followed closely behind the plow, plucking worms and grubs.

I like this life, I'm privileged to be here. All this could be mine someday. Bobbie and I could work it just like Dad and I do. The realization that Claude wouldn't live forever overpowered him. It was a sad thought, he knew deep in his heart how much he loved his Dad.

I'll stay here, there's no need to go anywhere. The field was a good half mile long. Danny spun the tractor 180 degrees, he gazed at the sea of black dirt before him.

"I wonder what Argentina's like. I could fly a twin, I know I could. There's just two engine gauges and two throttles. I could do it."

And so it went, north was stay, and south was Argentina. Back and forth all day, and the next day, and the next.

On Thursday at noon Claude and Danny parked their rigs under a lone oak tree. They cleaned the plows with a sharp short shovel, ate their bologna and cheese sandwiches and talked while sipping sweet iced tea.

"Dad, do you ever get bored out here?"

"No, son, I don't"

Claude kinda knew where this was going, he had been thinking I'm not pushing the issue for or against. It will have to be his decision. If I know anything, I know that."

"Well, I get bored. I kinda been thinking about that offer from Marie."

Claude felt goose bumps go up his forearms, he didn't know what caused it. Was it the mention of Marie or Argentina or both? Claude clearly did not like Marie, nor did he trust her. The past was too grueling and painful. He had prayed to forgive her and he thought he had. That is until she resurfaced, the new improved Marie.

"I had rather see you join the peace corps than to get mixed up with that woman."

"Why Dad, what's wrong with her?"

"It's a long story son. The Bible says to forgive those who hurt and sin against you. I have forgiven her, but the good book also says to stay away from those you know to be wicked and evil, choose righteous and good people to be around."

Danny understood what his Dad had just told him. There were definitely passages to the effect of what Claude had paraphrased.

On the other hand, how evil could this sweet old lady be. She's doing God's work, helping others.

They went back to work, both of them stewing over Argentina and Marie. Danny could tell by the look on his Dad's face, whatever happened between the two of them, his Dad had not forgotten or forgiven. He also knew in all his twenty two years, his Dad's ire was up. Better leave this alone, maybe Mom will fill in the details.

Friday night rolled around. Danny had taken a shower, put on his weekend clothes and was ready to hit the town. Claude was at the kitchen table, "How about some money Dad?"

Claude was already ahead of him, handing him the check before he got all the way to the rickety old dinette set. Danny looked at it. $125.00.

"Dad, a hundred and twenty five dollars, that's not even minimum wage. I put in over 65 hours this week."

"I know son. We should have discussed this before hand. Let me explain. I'm showing you on the farm books as farm labor. Once the crops are harvested I"ll give you a percentage of the profit."

"Dad, two years ago when it only rained twelve inches all year, there was no profit. I know I went to college and all, but ain't "a" percentage of nothing nothing?"

"Yes, Danny, farming is risky, a few bad years and you're out."

Danny threw his hands up and walked away, his back to his Dad saying," We're gonna talk about this."

Claude's only downfall was his tight fisted Irish green soul. He changed the oil in his farm equipment only four times a year. On two of those changes he would drain the old oil, run it through cheese cloth and put the same oil back in the equipment. His old '57 Plymouth wagon ran until it just flat wore out. Claude rolled it behind the barn saying he was going to have it overhauled. It was now the home for laying hens and rats.

When Claude ran the compress, he wore khaki pants and white shirts. Five pair total. The only thing that changed when he started farming were the shirts, they were now also khaki. Of course, Claude had other clothes, Sunday best, kinds of collections of various suits and sports jackets. All good quality, that would be foolish not to buy good quality.

Claude often thought Clara's spending was excessive, although after they married she never used a credit card again. The clothing and shopping were very rigid standards. Somewhat out of line with reality. Clara missed the shopping. They polarized in different directions. Claude at times could be down right cheap. Clara had been known to run through thousands in a single day. I guess, in part, that's why she was willing to forgive Marie. Not that she wanted to go back to being under her thumb, but she had truly appreciated the way Marie's "no limit" giving made her feel. Sometimes she really missed that, but lately Claude had become even more cautious with his money. Maybe it was this farm venture. Nevertheless, if they fought, it was over money. In the past that was rare, not quite so anymore.

Danny and Claude had finished the spring planting, the soybeans were shooting up and showing signs of good growth. Claude kept a close eye on all his crops, especially the "beans" as they were called. They were by far the most risky and profitable since soybean products were used in virtually everything in farm feed; cattle, hogs, horses, even chicken feed. Not to mention various food producers. From the commodity market to the farm they were simply referred to as "beans." On the farm it was called a "cash crop."

During the growing season when the plants were young and tender, aphids, grasshoppers, caterpillars, and the like could damage crops. Their damage was inevitable, there would always be some, the extent was the key. Claude visited each field several times daily, each spraying cost thousands of dollars, so he was on top of it. Walking to remote, random sections, closely examining a small group of individual plants while observing the obvious on the way to that particular location.

CHAPTER THIRTY ONE

Early on things looked great, timely rains, no major problems. Then one day Claude saw a small greenish tiny bug on the underside of some leaves. He collected them in lab like vials. Claude being fairly new to farming kept the county agriculture agent busy. He called him out for a visit.

Avery Lopez arrived in his county pick up. Avery was tall for a man of Latin descent, handsome in the Spanish tradition, dark, almost black eyes, with a full black moustache. His dress was meticulous, ostrich quill cowboy boots, a hand carved leather western belt with an oval silver buckle, an expensive western style hat ,he looked neat, a man with a knack for details.

Avery considered Claude a pain in the ass, but went out of his way to be friendly and helpful. Claude produced the vial from his pocket.

"What do you think about this?"

"Aphids" Avery replied without hesitation.

"Should I spray?" Claude quipped back in a nervous, short chatter.

"Let's go look at the fields, then I can tell you how bad it is, regardless, you'll need to spray."

Avery was a technical genius. He really thought to himself this guy is as green as these aphids.

Claude and Avery waded through the "beans." Avery stopped in about twenty five yards knelt down and began to examine a single plant. He spent a good five minutes alone on this plant. His exam almost complete, suddenly he pulled the entire plant out of the ground and began to closely look at the roots.

Avery discarded the plant, slapped his hands together removing the dirt. He went straight to his pocket producing a business card that read, "Aces" Crop Dusting Service, all types aerial spraying.

Claude read the card.

"I have spraying equipment. I'll spray myself."

Avery came back almost before Claude completed his sentence. "If you do you'll lose this entire crop. Aphids produce so fast by the time you finish the first round of spraying you'll have to begin again. You could end up spraying here all summer, that would eat up any profit you could possibly make. It's simple economics."

Claude stood in his sloppy wrinkled trousers, sweat marks outlining his underarms and part of his chest. " Damn, Gaud damn" is all Claude could say. He watched Avery drive away.

"Why doesn't that damn Mexican sweat?"

Claude was on the phone to "Aces" within the hour.

"Can't get to you until next week a female voice replied. You'll need to mark the outlines of your fields so we'll know where to spray. It would be a good idea to have someone watch us the first time we spray to make sure we are in the right place. We wouldn't want to spray someone else's property." a slight chuckle from the female voice.

"OK, how do we do that?" Claude replied, angry at her weak joke.

"It's simple, drive to the field you want sprayed. Tape the top of your vehicle with an "X", once we start spraying watch the wind, then drive to where you're up wind of the chemical coming out of the plane."

"Sir, how many acres?"

"About twelve hundred in beans. How much is that going to cost?"

"It's about ten dollars per acre."

"My God, that's twelve thousand dollars."

"Yes, it's expensive. Do you want to think about it?"

"No. What day and time will you be here?" Claude was angry.

He wished he was in his element back at the compress. He wondered if Modeena would let him buy it back, then thought a second time. *All my money is in this farm, it's not a liquid asset. It could take years to sell it.*

The week passed like a jail sentence, all he and Danny could do was wait. Danny could see visible changes in his Dad, the stress was silently taking its toll. Claude looked tired and was not sleeping well.

The spray day finally arrived. A short Hispanic man arrived at dawn, on the side of his white pick up truck was a decal of a bi-plane laying out puffs of little white clouds, "Aces" in bold script beneath it.

Danny and Claude led the way. Two planes arrived, once positioned, they began to spray. Danny watched intently as they raced across the field, at the end one would break right, the other left, climb abruptly and do a gentle figure eight and return for another run. Danny was mesmerized.

They moved to another field. The planes left, the Hispanic man said in broken English, "They go get more chemical."

This was Danny's chance. "How much do you pay those pilots?"

"I dun know, maybe mucho."

The planes returned and the choreographed performance began again.

"Don't even think about it," Claude said.

Danny knew his Dad knew what he was thinking. Danny backed off, he didn't want to worry his Dad.

It took two full days to complete the spraying. Danny had called "Aces" asking if they could use another pilot.

"Sure," the female voice replied. Danny thought he could detect a slight Spanish accent.

Her name was Loraine Danny found the next day. She was Spanish, or at least looked it; long dark almost black hair, dark penetrating eyes. When she stood to go to the file cabinet for his application he noticed she was very well proportioned, large breasts, Danny guessed a size C. The best thing about her body was her butt, Danny thought to himself that's probably the best butt I have ever seen. Actually she was extremely feminine in every regard, just the way God would make a perfect woman. Her waist was tiny which made her other assets that much more attractive.

"You look to young to be a pilot," Loraine said as she handed Danny the application and a pen.

"Well, I'm not, I'm a licensed pilot," Danny said in a defensive tone.

"Hey, I didn't mean to piss you off," Loraine quickly retorted.

Danny took the paperwork and a seat near her on a little work table next to her desk. "You're too good looking to piss me off. Got a boyfriend?"

"Yeah, about half a dozen. You'll have to get in line."

"Is that an invitation?" Danny asked giving his crooked grin.

Loraine bit her lower lip in what Danny perceived as the sexiest thing she could have done.

"Maybe" acting shy which she wasn't in the least.

Danny completed his application which would have taken about ten minutes in an hour and a half. Flirting, and talking, generally getting to know each other. Almost a first date.

Danny stared at all the empty spaces where the experience boxes appeared on the one page document. He tossed it on her desk, trying to be as cool as possible.

Loraine picked it up immediately. "My Dad's not going to use you."

"Now how do you know that?" still trying to maintain what he thought he had established, but hadn't.

"Dad gets ten applications a month with guys that have thousands of hours. Who are you kiddin, it says here you went to college, have eighty hours and have worked three months for your Dad. Good luck with that."

Danny turned red with a blush that came from nowhere.

"Oh that's cute. Our people don't blush."

"What do you mean "our people?"

"We're from Brazil" she said in perfect English, until she got to Brazil then switched to some language Danny couldn't quite place. Somehow he knew that she had pronounced it correctly.

"Since I have some time invested here, I just want to let you know I'm getting in line. When can I have my shot?" Danny said the last word with a heavy sexual undertone.

Loraine, sitting at her desk, rested her chin on her thumb, tucking it just a bit as she rolled her beautiful dark eyes up toward the ceiling beyond and above where Danny was standing.

"I'll let you know."

Danny was losing points fast. He couldn't remember a girl looking completely through him. He felt like a fly or some other insignificant pest. Danny made it out the ripped screen door, he looked back like a bandit would in a robbery.

"Gaud dammit, I only annoyed her."

That's not at all what I wanted, he thought, as he cranked his second hand pick up and sped away.

Danny's phone did not ring, but he often had more interest in Loraine than he did the pilot job. He would call her every day under the guise of the job query. His real intentions were certainly not honorable, well maybe they were, after all he wasn't asking for something that wasn't natural for a young man his age.

He would generally begin his calls with, "I don't want to annoy you," with a definite emphasis on "annoy." Loraine would giggle and say "Hi Danny," then they would have a long talk, the next day, even longer. Something was happening, Danny was not sure quite what.

One day Danny called and out of nowhere he said, "I'd marry you right now if you'd have me."

Loraine gave in. "You can have your date, maybe then you'll leave me alone." She didn't mean it.

Claude and Danny had seen it through the aphid ordeal everything was looking up at the farm. The beans looked good, they should do well this year. The harvest was drawing near, the next week they would rent equipment and hope Claude's second hand peanut thrasher would hold up.

Danny asked Claude at supper Friday night, "Did you know you wanted to marry Mom when you first met her, I mean...."

Claude was stoic and cautious. "Why do you ask?"

"I've met this girl, tonight's our first date. I've had lots of dates, and quite a few girl friends, I've just never felt like I do about this girl."

"Oh, I see. Would this be Loraine by any chance?"

"How did you know that?"

"Well apparently she feels pretty strongly about you too. You know the other night when I sent you to Slidell for parts, she called asking for you."

"Really? Why didn't you tell me she called?"

"I had a gut instinct, it wouldn't be the right thing to do. Your mother's curiosity is rubbing off on me."

"Oh." Is all Danny had to say, with a puzzled look.

An hour later Danny was where Loraine had told him to come. The office shack by the runway where they first met. A house was up the road, Danny could see the lights burning. He thought maybe that's where she lived, it was the closest house after all. Danny waited. After awhile, fifteen or twenty minutes, a small single made an approach, touched down as smooth as silk and taxied up fairly close to the shack. He was impressed by the landing, he had slammed a few hard landings, but was much better now than before.

Danny studied the plane, he thought it was an old Taylor Craft, a tail dragger. He had never flown one of those, all his time was in Cessna tricycle type landing gears, he told himself, "I could handle that."

A figure appeared and started toward the shack, closer now, he could make out it was a woman, closer it was Loraine.

Danny grabbed her and kissed her. It was wonderful, she kissed him back. "Ain't love a wonderful thing?" Danny said.

Loraine looked at him deeply but said nothing.

In a short while, Danny said, "Well what's your pleasure? What do you want to do?"

"Ever fly one of those?" pointing to the tail dragger, Loraine said.

"No" Danny replied. "What is it anyway?"

"It's my Dad's 1949 Taylor Craft, he used to give flying lessons in it in Brazil."

"Yeah, I'll give it a go, right now?" Danny was a bit apprehensive, yet willing to go ahead, he certainly didn't want Loraine to think he lacked machismo.

Danny and Loraine walked toward the plane, it was dark now.

Danny eased close, the plane was unlike any other he had flown. There were two seats, back to back, like something out of the Red Baron era. Danny had always flown planes where the seats were arranged side by side. He felt a certain comfort in that, being able to see the person next to you, make eye contact, watch their movements, see their instruments. Suddenly he felt "butterflies", his stomach in a tight churning knot. Danny welcomed the dark, he didn't want to give away his nervousness and tension.

"Which seat?" Danny said.

"It doesn't matter, they are identical." Danny caught a distinct, almost heavy Spanish accent.

Danny climbed in the back, Loraine gave a smirking, condescending grin, then took the remaining front seat. It was a closed cockpit, that it is not open to the elements, the only differences were the back to back seating, and the instrumentation.

Loraine said, "I'll start it, then you take over." As soon as the engine turned over and caught on, there was utter silence, except that of the engine. Danny felt lost, only the dim lights giving him just enough illumination to see a lever on the left marked in faded half chipped off paint labeled "FLAPS." The other one, the one on the right, must be the throttle. Danny set the flaps at what he thought to be zero, grabbed what he thought to be the throttle and shoved it forward. The engine groaned, the plan began to move.

Yeah, Danny thought, that's the throttle. He taxied toward the end of the runway, pushed left rudder pedal, the plane veered left, then the right, it went right. OK that's the same, Danny thought. The stick between his legs felt awkward, out of place, the Cessna's at Mississippi State had steering wheel type yokes. This was definitely different.

At the end of the runway Danny spun the plane into the slight almost insignificant wind. He yelled at Loraine over the engine noise, "What's the power setting?"

Loraine held up her right hand barely visible against the faint glow from her instruments. Two fingers, then five.

Danny's mind raced, two-five. OK. 2500.

Danny toed the pedals, holding the brakes, the engine RPM gauge slowly climbed 1000, 1500, 2000, 2250, 2500. The engine sounded louder than any he had ever heard. Was this thing gonna fly apart right here on the ground? Danny took a deep breath and let the brakes go. The little plane hopped to life, like a flushed rabbit, the plane left the ground quickly, right after Danny felt the tail come off the ground. This thing is fast, nimble, responsive, Danny thought, the stick was touchy, very touchy.

They made several slow circles around the field. Then they headed south. Danny yelled, "What altitude?" One finger followed by three quick fists.

1000, a thousand Danny figured.

They flew for about twenty minutes, Danny constantly scanning the gauges. He was particularly concerned about the fuel, it was below a quarter of a tank. The moon was quartering, bright enough to see parts of the ground or an occasional car or truck headlights below. But not the horizon.

Danny was growing concerned, could he find the runway? He was low on fuel, what if he couldn't? Had Loraine been paying attention?

Danny did at 180 degree, and headed the compass needle north, he should see the runway in twenty minutes or so. Twenty minutes passed, the watch on Danny's arm his only clue to where he was.

Twenty five minutes, the fuel gauge was bouncing off empty.

Two hands appeared in front of Danny fluttering like a pigeon about to land.

Danny was still trying to put together the meaning of the signal.

The stick that Danny had gingerly held, almost coddled, slammed forward, the plane nosed over sharply. Danny, not thinking, grabbed for it, like trying to retrieve a dropped coin.

One fluttering hand.

Danny realized Loraine was flying the plane.

She took it down very quickly, yet extremely smooth, in a rapidly descending figure eight.

Loraine landed the plane and taxied out, cutting the engine. They both emerged from the plane. Danny was green around the gills, he welcomed the darkness, again hiding his embarrassment.

"Where did you learn to fly like that?" Danny stammered.

"Who do you think was flying the second plane when you're fields were sprayed?"

Danny reached for his forehead, placing all his fingertips and thumb in the center just above his brow ridge.

"It was me, stupid" Loraine declared.

Danny, struggling, finally said, "What are we gonna do for the rest of our first date?"\

"You could take me to dinner. I'm hungry."

"Where would you like to go?" Danny asked.

"I like fish, it fills me up, and I can eat a whole lot of it without gaining any weight" Loraine said shyly.

"Weight, you got to be kidding me, you're perfect."

"Your kidding yourself if you think I look this way without proper diet and exercise. I eat fish most meals and I jog three miles every morning. You know you got to have a plan and stick with it."

"Yeah," Danny shrugged, knowing the flight he just piloted would have ended in disaster

if Loraine had not rescued him at the last minute. The thought was in the back of his head, Loraine knew that all too well.

Loraine said, "So how did you like the Taylor?"

"It was a trip, why didn't you let me land it?"

Loraine was quick to respond. "Well, let's see. You didn't set your altimeter, or ask the take off RPM, or ask the heading, or ask how much fuel, or ask where the hell we were when I knew you were totally lost. Maybe landing a plane you've never flown before at night, with a totally different landing gear...."

"Whoa, Whoa! Was I that bad?" Danny interrupted.

"Yes, worse than I expected" with a heavy Spanish accent. Danny had begun to notice when Loraine got a little excited it was more pronounced.

Danny pulled into what he thought was the only fish place in Slidell. Katfish Kave.

"No, No, I know a better place, will you take directions?" Maybe Loraine was relaxing, the accent now seemed very natural and sexy.

"Yeah, I'll take di'rec'she'on," Danny replied fooling around, teasing her accent a bit.

"Don't make fun of me," Loraine acting angry replied.

They both laughed and Danny drove the back roads taking directions, carefully following them without hesitation or comment.

Out of nowhere appeared a Mexican style restaurant. Very quaint, adobe style, heavy wooden timbers hanging out the front and over the open court yard.

"El Golfo" in small letters, too small to see from the Farm to Market road, stenciled above the door. The bar was busy, the restaurant too.

"Where did all these people park?" Danny asked.

"Out back, you were lucky to get a place in front. Someone must have just left." Loraine no more than got those words from her mouth when the hostess appeared in a bright red and yellow dress with flowing rings of Spanish style ruffles.

"Loraine," the hostess shouted over the crowd chatter. It was obvious they knew each other as friends.

Loraine introduced Danny to Marguerite. Explaining they were new, but good friends.

Marguerite led them to a table in the back. Once seated, Marguerite said, "Your Papa was here earlier, he already left though."

"Oh, I guess he's got an early day tomorrow." Loraine said, as if this place were her second home.

"The usual wine?"

"Si, por fa'vor," Loraine said. The wine arrived, a deep mellow red Merlot. Danny and Loraine drank and talked, the more they drank, the more each opened to the other. By the time the waitress took their orders, the bottle was almost empty.

"Another bottle of wine?" the waitress asked.

"No," Loraine said, not giving Danny a chance to respond. "We'll both have the whole red snapper, baked potatoes, and the extra large salad with two side plates." Loraine placed the orders like a high ranking general.

"And to drink?" the waitress asked.

"Aqua, grande aqua," Loraine replied.

Danny was impressed, Loraine was way a head of him. He hadn't even had time to look the menu over.

This forceful, aggressive, take charge woman was a new thing to Danny. He had plenty of dates in college where he always asked the lady what she wanted, then placed the order for the two of them. Besides, he thought Spanish women were supposed to be submissive, quiet, even reticent. "Boy was I wrong," Danny thought. Then he thought again, "Why not, it's like the plane. I don't know what the hell I'm doing. I thought white wine went with fish. Hell, I don't even like fish."

Loraine and Danny polished off the remains of the deep red, about a half glass each, it was hard to tell exactly how much was left in the straw lined bottle so Danny poured slowly. They didn't have much to say now, the wine working it's magic. The two held hands across the table, Loraine gently stroking, with her hand and her eyes. Danny had never felt this relaxed, and comfortable before. Never with anyone ever. His heart was hers.

The fish arrived, breaking the spell. Danny looked down in disbelief, it was the largest fish he'd ever seen. It's head and tail overhanging the oversized platter. An eye, a huge fish eye, staring up from the fish corpse, made Danny feel as though he was about to eat the family dog.

He quickly stole a glance at Loraine, she had already begun to dissect her dinner. Danny slid one of the lemon slices over the fish eye, thinking I can't do this with him looking at me. It worked, although the moved lemon slice revealed lacerations scored into the side of the pink flesh.

Danny pricked a hole into the side and dug out a fork full of the white flaky, expertly prepared main course. He thought he was in heaven. "This must be the best thing I've ever eaten," he told Loraine. The dinner was perfect, the company even better.

Danny took Loraine back to her plane. She said, "I'll just spend the night in the field shack, there's a cot in there. I can't get any fuel until tomorrow."

Danny got out of his pick up hoping for an invitation, his intentions were quite natural.

They walked toward the shack, holding hands. Once at the door Danny kissed her. "Any chance of me coming inside?"

"No," Loraine made clear the boundaries. Danny never doubted she would.

CHAPTER THIRTY TWO

Summer was taking its last breath, gasping for cooler days. The sugar maple in the De Moss front yard was renovated into a bright crimson red. The "beans" were a welcome profit to the farm, Danny had no doubt Claude would give him his cut. The problem was, cut of what? Claude kept the books and Danny only had a half ass clue as to how many bushels were produced. He would be forced to trust Claude, normally Danny would, but if Claude had any major flaws in his character, it would be money. Everything about money that was bad, hoarding, stashing away for rainy days. It could come a flood and the money would float away before Claude would pry it from his clenched, tight ass fists.

Danny tried to check during the harvest how many beans per acre they were harvesting. Soybeans were taken to the peanut house and weighed. A slip of paper stating the weight was produced each time a buggy of beans crossed the scale. The problem was Claude made certain Danny didn't go to the scales, keeping him busy with the harvest out in the hot parched fields. Danny saw red flags, smelled a rat, whatever you want to call it. He even felt guilty about not trusting his Dad, it was the look on his face when he returned from the scales more than anything. Claude may have been a cheating horrible miser, but he was an even worse liar.

There had been confrontations, Danny was assertive enough; asking to see the slips even asking to take buggies to the scales. Claude always rebuffed his inquiries and requests. "We'll see when its all done, one acre may make half as much as another," Claude would say.

All the beans were over the scales. Danny had checked around the farm, just to make sure Claude wasn't holding out on him. Hoarding, hiding buggies, if stored properly in a dry place there was no reason Claude couldn't run them across later. Matter of fact, many farmers did just that, waiting until prices changed or a need arose for quick cash. It was as simple as selling a calf or pig.

The peanut house operator, Floyd, had strict orders not to divulge anything to anyone unless they had the tax number. Not just the De Moss farm, any producers, it was policy. Danny would have to find another way not to get screwed. He felt a show down was coming.

Mostly black laborers worked the peanut house, moving buggies, auguring, and shoveling, the dirty work. Danny didn't know any of them, but he knew who did. He called Modeena explaining his plight.

"Good Gaud, dat Mr. Claude do be as tight as da bark on a tree," Modeena replied. "But dat ain't no problem. I'll find out fer ya TODAY."

Modeena called back in thirty minutes.

"Ok, I got the figures fer ya"

Danny thanked Modeena, but he didn't get away without a sermon.

"Ya know, ya gotz to trust in the Lord. Even if Mr. Claude is doin' bad things, ya gotz to forgive him. Causen if you don't, den you a sinnin'."

"Yes'um Modeena, I know that, but I don't think the Lord would approve of me gettin' screwed either."

"You right Mr. Danny. I raised you right, You just trust in the Lord, you just trust in the Lord, you heara."

"Yes, Mam" Danny had a sick feeling, betrayal possibly the worst emotion surged through him cutting him to pieces, killing his soul.

The figures were way off, not even half of the amount of buggies Claude had told Danny was true.

Danny actually made his way to the yard, so sick and upset he started to vomit. His hands were shaking, stabbed through the heart, by someone who was supposed to love him.

Now it wasn't the money, it was the pain. How could he make it stop? Would he ever stop hurting, would he ever feel love for his Dad again? They had been so close, now Danny questioned that, had his Dad been playing a role? Like in a play, was his love an act?

Rapid fire thoughts went through his head. When he held me as a baby, played games with me, tutored me, that was all an act. He's never loved me or he wouldn't do this to me.

Danny slowed his thoughts, they were getting out of hand. A classic over reaction, "Yeah, this is a classic," Danny told himself.

Danny tried to be methodical, but he was too upset. He rinsed his mouth out and spit in the sink, flushing water over his face. That seemed to cool him off a bit. I'll write down what I'm feeling and see if I'm over reacting. Danny faced a note lined piece of white paper and sat at the kitchen table. The table where he had eaten most meals of his life.

How do I feel and why?

1. Hurt. Why? Betrayal.

2. Betrayed. Why? My Dad doesn't love me.

3. My Dad doesn't love me. Why? I failed him or he me.

4. I failed him or he me. Why? I didn't deserve to reap rewards, or he didn't think I deserved them.

5. This is crap. My Dad, the Christian, the loving father, has fucked me.

Danny broke the #2 pencil, crumbling it in his hands, anger coursed through his veins. He went to his room, and began to pack. Some of his things he hadn't even unpacked since college. Winter coats, light jackets, and sweaters. Where Danny was going he wouldn't have need for that sort of stuff. South Texas, the Rio Grande Valley. He hoped Loraine's offer still stood and her Dad would put him to work.

Claude pulled in the drive shortly after sundown. Danny waited, stewing.

"How much am I going to get for this year's crop?" Danny asked angrily.

"We need to talk about that son." Claude knew Danny was upset, but he didn't know he had checked up on his buggy counts.

Claude started to explain, "Last year was not a good year. There would need to be adjustments made for the 25% he had promised."

Danny had figured correctly, Claude was crawfishing out of the deal.

"Just write me a check," Danny yelled.

Claude had known for months he wasn't going to honor his promise. Actually he had worked quite hard at his devious deceptions. After all Claude had raised the boy, fed, and clothed him, sent him to college. Hell, bought his old white ford pick up truck.

Claude pulled his check book out and began to write. Reluctantly handing the check to Danny.

"Five thousand dollars," Danny exclaimed. "It should be at least ten thousand," Danny screamed.

"It is what it is," Claude said calmly, peering over the top of his five and dime reading glasses.

Danny stuffed the check in his shirt pocket. If he ever wanted to hit his Dad it was now. Danny was mustering all his resolve not to hit him. He wanted to in the worst way, instead he turned and walked out the door.

The Ford F-150 made a trail of dust as it sped down the dusty lane. Danny checked his rear view, the De Moss house was behind him.

Danny had Loraine's letters and general whereabouts, not knowing her exact location.

A day and a half later, the white Ford roamed McAllen, Texas. After some questioning Danny managed to get directions to the return address Loraine had given.

It was almost identical to the setup in Elmbrook, there was a small runway and a scattering of out buildings. He drove around looking each one over thoroughly. After thirty minutes or so he spotted the address, hand painted on an old aircraft hangar. He peeked through a crack in the hangar doors which were secured with a heavy chain and pad lock. Danny checked the lock to make sure it was locked and not positioned to look so. He banged on the door with as much force as possible without hurting his fist. No one came, the place looked abandoned, except for the glow from an unshaded light bulb far in the back. Danny turned to leave, just then Loraine came from around the side of the building.

They kissed, Loraine was as happy to see Danny as he was to see her. Back in Elmbrook the two had become constant companions, it hurt both of them to leave each other. Whether they knew it or not, they were soul mates, made by the Grace of God.

The hot summer sun in McAllen rekindled the flames of passion and romance. They really had never flickered. Loraine's Dad was willing to put Danny to work spraying, Federico needed and wanted another wing man, he had never been comfortable with Loraine, she took too many chances and he worried about her.

The first day of work Federico appeared out of the pre-dawn haze, walking closer to Danny and extending his hand. Their hand shakes were firm and solid. Immediately Danny liked Federico, he spoke with a heavy Spanish accent. Sometimes so much so Danny couldn't understand what he had just said.

To Danny Federico looked like a tough retired Hispanic welter weight boxer. He was quick with his movements, his body fit the boxer build. Maybe a few pounds heavier than fight weight. A handsome face that had seen some hard blows. For fifty years old he was in remarkable shape. Danny was about to see why.

"Today we start. We run to the end and back." Federico pointed toward the end of the runway. Without hesitation Federico lit out, running, it took Danny by surprise. He thought he had come to fly. Federico's white tennis shoes were disappearing into the predawn darkness. Danny sprinted to catch up. They ran silently, up and down the taxi way. Danny was getting winded, Federico tossed two fingers into the air after they had jogged for over an hour.

"Dos Mas" Federico said. Now Danny knew where Loraine's had signals had originated.

Sure enough, they made two more trips. Danny was young, didn't smoke and usually limited his alcohol reasonably. Federico was physically kicking his ass. Danny stopped, then started walking on the last leg into the spot where they began.

Danny sheepishly approached Federico who was now doing push-ups. Without uttering a word Federico continued, jumping jacks, squat thrusts, and crunches. Federico stopped, Danny thought "finally." A boxer style jump rope emerged from under Federico's sweat shirt. He jumped rope expertly, cris crosses, pepper, he went on and on, one foot then the other. The performance ended with a both feet walking pepper.

Danny sat on the ground exhausted his arm wrapped round his knees. Federico un-winded was sweating profusely but had stopped and was looking at Danny.

"You outa shape, amigo" Federico said. Danny nodded in agreeance, "yeah" was all he could manage to say.

"Now we fly," Federico announced.

Danny followed. The stearman biplane was a bright canary yellow. The set up was the same as the Taylor Craft, back to back seats, a tail wheel except this one was rigged with spray equipment. Danny helped push it out of the hangar.

They did a short pre-flight inspection, Federico mostly pointing out things related to the sprayers. Federico climbed in the back seat, Danny took the front. It looked different from up here, hey, Danny thought, I can't take hand signals from here.

"Who's flying this thing?" Danny asked.

"You Amigo" Federico said.

"Where to, what do you want me to do?"

"Just take her up, get the feel of her." Danny felt more plane under him the minute he throttled the giant radial engine in front of him, he sensed it. Power, more power than the tiny engines he knew.

The plane responded in a burst of power and speed. Danny had anticipated, somehow it had fallen short. The surge of power and force, the speed and quickness matched Federico. The controls were the same quick, fast, almost knee jerk responsive. Danny felt a rush, maybe for the first time in a plane. The puddle jumpers he had been flying didn't do this for him. He climbed as he was accustomed and trained to do. Altitude in training meant safety, time to buy in case of an emergency. Engine out drills; put the nose down and guide safely to earth. Time to find a field to land in, time to get the plane under control in a shallow gliding attitude. All that was out the window, Federico beat his open palm on the plane behind Danny, he swivelled his neck far enough to see Federico's hand, it pointed down.

Danny banked and drove even though he was only 500 feet above the ground. Every pilot instinct and training was going against his grain, dive and short turns close to the ground. Danny learned fast, when you've got altitude, you have time; when you don't, you don't.

The ground raced up, Danny caught on, he was training to be a crop duster right. Federico pounded the small space between the two seats again, he pointed down.

Gaud damn, Danny thought, I just cleared that power line. Again Federico pounded; down. Danny made another pass at the row crop below him. Too fast to recognize what was growing there. Danny forced the massive engine and wings lower, he had never been this close to the ground before at speed, flying speed, that is, not landing speed. Danny could swear the wheels on the stearman were slapping the tops of the unknown vegetation.

And so it went, unrelenting as the morning workout. Try harder, do it again; try harder, do it again. It was redundant, purposeful, exhilarating, torturous.

Federico slammed his palm one last time. Just as with Loraine, the controls were snatched away, like someone unaware.

Federico landed the yellow canary.

"I thought you said you could fly?"

"I can, it's just everything about it, thats, thats different," Danny stammered.

"Be here manyana, Amigo. That is if that's what you want." Federico overemphasized the "that" mocking Danny in a playful way.

Two weeks later, Federico decided Danny was ready to make some denior. He had learned a lot, his responsiveness and quickness much improved. He was also beginning to get a chiseled, leaner look. So was his wallet, Federico hadn't paid him a dime. Danny didn't blame him, after all they both knew he wasn't ready at the start of the training.

Danny's five thousand was dwindling and he was happy tomorrow would stop the financial bleed. Soon he would ask Loraine to marry him.

CHAPTER THIRTY THREE

The valley provided year around steady employment. The problem was there was big money to be made when situations arose. If the Lubbock, Texas area experienced infestation problems, buckets of money could be made. Federico kept his ear to the ground, ready to jump at any chance for big money. The way he figured, crop dusters took plenty of chances, hell just flying was a chance. Why not optimize the risk reward.

Sure enough one morning Danny arrived to find the two Stearmans on a trailer, wings carefully packed along the sides.

"What's going on?" Danny asked.

"The Texas high plains, ever pest known to cotton is eating them up." Federico happily announced, rubbing his hands together.

"Go get your gear, if you're going."

"Yeah, OK" Danny exclaimed. Danny quickly packed and picked up Loraine.

"Where exactly are we going?" Danny asked.

"A little town called Roscoe. My Dad started there twenty-nine years ago. It's an easy way to make lots of money fast. Very few trees and power lines, only an occasional oil pump jack or drilling rig. We could make fifty thousand dollars each in a couple of months."

Loraine looked questioningly towards Danny. Would the money nudge Danny closer to popping the question? Loraine was most definitely in love and so was Danny. Danny drove on in silence thinking the money is not in the bank yet.

That night they drove from the valley to Austin, spent the night in a rat-hole motel, leaving at dawn the next morning. Roscoe, Danny found, was quite a haul. Federico stopped at least every other rest stop checking hauling straps, looking for any movement or shifting of his precious cargo. Danny would cuss, "Gaud damn if it hasn't moved yet, it's not going to!" Loraine always defended her Dad. "It's his lifeblood on those trailers, just go along with him, the planes are his life."

"No, he's got more than that," Danny said. "God is with him."

Loraine thought a moment, thinking about what Danny had just said. Then in a slow comforting tone said, "Yes, my Dad has always had God with him. He prays every night. I hear him sometimes, he prays for strength, guidance, direction and the forgiveness of his sins. Sometimes he drinks too much, so I don't know what other than that his sins could be. He asks God to bless my Mother and sisters, to watch over them and to protect them."

"Well, that's a nice prayer," Danny said.

"Yes, it is Danny," Loraine put her head on Danny's shoulder. In a matter of minutes she was asleep.

Danny drove on, west toward Roscoe. The sunset was brilliant as he passed through Sweetwater. It was still, pink wispy cotton candy clouds sprawled above the moon scape terrain with an occasional cactus and clumps of stunted mesquites. Danny thought "Sweetwater, what a nice name." It wouldn't fit anywhere else. Danny at last was at peace with himself, he thought about his Dad, how he had stormed off. Maybe he needed to say the same prayer. Maybe he had found the place God had intended him to fit. In love with Loraine forever.

Danny gently shook Loraine, she opened her eyes barely enough to catch the sunset. "Oh Danny, it's beautiful."

"Loraine, will you marry me?"

"Of course I will, but you'll have to ask Papa."

Danny pressed on into Roscoe following the two canaries. Federico pulled into a dusty truck stop, parking the rig well to the north side of the parking area. Federico went inside and came out shortly.

"We'll spend the night here, I have permission."

"Ok" Danny said knowing Federico was not about to leave the rig.

"Federico," Danny shouted. "Do I have permission to marry Loraine?"

Federico had already started walking back towards the planes. He stopped dead in his tracks, it seemed he was frozen for a few seconds, then he slowly turned. Motioning Danny as he always did with hand signals, "Come here Amigo."

Danny approached cautiously, suddenly he felt threatened. Federico was not smiling.

Danny stood in the whirling dust face to face with his friend and mentor. Federico spoke first, "Yes, but only under certain conditions. You must marry in the church. You must raise your children in the church. You must never strike her, if you do, I come for you."

Federico was now tapping Danny on his chest with his index finger. Danny looked down at the finger, he didn't like it, his temper flared. He wanted to slap Federico's hand away. Federico now pressed the finger firmly against his chest.

"There is one more thing Amigo. You must believe in God."

"I do, I will," Danny managed to say.

"No, No, you daunt." Federico stared intently into Danny's eyes searching for truth.

"Federico, I do believe in God," Danny exclaimed.

"No, no, you daunt," Federico returned to his truck slamming the door shut.

Danny was bewildered, but proud he hadn't lost his temper. It seemed Federico was deliberately goading him. Danny cussed under his breath on his way back to Loraine.

"Why did that crazy son of a bitch do that? Do I have his gaud damn permission or not?" Danny got in his truck and slammed the door shut.

"What was all that about?" Loraine asked.

"Nothin'" Danny muttered, "nothin'."

A few days passed and things had settled a bit between Danny and Federico. The first day of crop dusting wasn't much different than the valley with the single exception of the vastness of the crops. They could easily get three sometimes four times the amounts of chemical down. It was hot, stinky work. Danny couldn't help but draw parallels between Claude's tractors and Federico's canaries. Up and down, back and forth, it was plowing the air.

The days built time and experience, all Danny could think about was the money. He tallied his earnings mentally , if he could come out with twenty five grand they would marry. Danny had gotten very comfortable, relaxed actually. He trusted the yellow canary. The power was always there, he had grown to rely on it, almost take it for granted.

The canary returned to the make shift landing strip, loaded maximum chemical, and popped back in the air. In ten minutes it was laying down a streak of misting steam like fog. Suddenly, out of nowhere, before him was a strand of power lines, he had known they were there. A mental lapse, a mind trick, carelessness, hypnotized by redundancy. Danny yanked the stick back hard. It was too late, the huge propellor ripped the wires, chopping down the big radial engine. The engine stuttered, coughing, gasping for air and fuel. The canary began to sink, the wheels now past the power lines were popping the tops off the two foot high stalks of cotton. Danny managed to get his hand on the throttle, ease the stick back.. The engine hacked on, trying to regain it's lost power, a decade of his young life passed before him. Please come up, come up, he begged the canary. At last his prayer was answered. The engine still tossing off random pieces of chopped up wire. Danny didn't panic. The canary shouldered up through the head wind. "I'm sinking. I'm sinking, don't stall," Danny whispered to himself.

Normally the figure eight and return run would begin. Danny climbed and climbed. A thousand feet felt comfortable. Danny looked down his legs were shaking uncontrollably119, blood was dripping in his lap and down on his thighs. "Where's that coming from?" Danny tried to think. He could feel his pulse pounding in his head. Danny started to check for parts, parts of himself. His free hand began the search. Forehead, nose, mouth, ears, OK. Where's this blood coming from? The hand was shaking still trying to regain a semblance of motor control. A sharp barb, the hand had found warm, wet liquid. Danny continued to search, a piece of wire was sticking through his right cheek just below the outer part of his eye. Danny's breathing was shallow, rapid; a lightheadedness set in, "Don't hyperventilate," he said aloud.

The ten minutes back, was an hour a second. Time died, it seemed forever. Danny landed, cut his engine and sat, looking down on his shaking legs. He grabbed them with both hands trying to quell his adrenaline attack.

Danny sat in the plane twenty minutes or so, he didn't really know. Federico returned, landed and started to walk to Danny. By this time Danny had managed to exhaust himself from his fear, well at least his legs had stopped shaking on the outside. Inside his nerves were still jumping.

"What the hell happened?" Federico shouted. Danny, shell shocked, managed to tell.

"Are you hurt anywhere else?" Federico asked.

"No, I don't think so" Danny answered mustering enough courage not to look too bad.

Federico was checking the prop, it was chipped in several places. He left and went to the truck, returning with a step ladder and a pair of plyers. A fifth of whiskey tucked under his arm.

"Sit down," Federico said after unfolding the ladder next to the engine. Danny sat, Federico poured some of whiskey over the wire and entrance exit punctures. "Hold still" Federico ordered. The plyers gently tugging the skin outward away from his eye. Federico released the plyers letting the bloody strip of wire fall to the ground. He doused more whiskey on the wound. "That's gonna leave a scar, Amigo," Federico said, handing the whiskey to Danny. He took a long draw off the bottle, a deep breath, then another long draw.

"Now Amigo, now you believe in God." Federico declared.

CHAPTER THIRTY FOUR

Two weeks later Danny called home. "Dad, Loraine and I are getting married." There was a hesitation, then Claude yelled, "Clara, Danny and Loraine are getting married."

Without warning Danny was quickly speaking with Clara, her aggressive, pushy, take charge, no one can do it better than me attitude had struck gold.

"Oh Dear, a wedding, how exciting." Clara was in full plumage. Danny could see her aglow with wings spread.

"Let me talk to Loraine."

Danny had wanted to talk to his Dad, ask permission to come home and marry in the church. Instead he was sitting on the couch watching Loraine answer a battery of questions. Somehow he felt like a child that had turned the handle on a jack in the box, watching its little head waggle back and forth after the eruption.

Danny sat thinking, I love my mother, but not this side of her. He knew, at times, how kind and loving she could be. This would not be one of them.

Danny and Loraine approached the DeMoss house. Danny drove slowly, taking in each tree, every detail of the house. Childhood memories flooded his soul, how happy he had been here. Modeena, cap guns, Salem's, peach switches, incredible love.

Claude and Clara stepped onto the porch to greet their guests. Danny grabbed their only worn out battered suitcase in one hand and Loraine's in the other. He walked slowly, deliberately, toward them; no Modeena, no Bobby, no smile or slap on the back from Claude. Just a hollow, "Welcome, come in" from Clara.

Danny eyed the foreign interior of the house, the bannister he slid down, the dinette set, the old couch and chairs. His brain told him it was home, he could smell it, feel it, take comfort in it. His heart knew it was not so. There was no love or joy in it. A stranger lost in memories.

The wedding would be next Saturday. Danny wanted it as quick and as painless as possible. Loraine agreed, and was willing to let Clara take over the details knowing there was no stopping her.

Danny and Claude had several talks, they were strained and awkward. Each admitting mistakes on their parts. It was clear to Danny irrevocable damage, maybe even irritation, was lying in a shallow grave. Danny knew not to ask the questions he had come to ask. When Claude said, "Well son, what are your plans?" No offers to stay were extended. Danny had planned on the cold shoulder treatment and answered, "Brazil, Loraine wants to go home."

"I see, what will you do there?" Claude asked as if cued.

"Fly." Danny answered, knowing he had no job prospects.

Again, Claude asked for no details, another sign to Danny he was not welcome back home. Hell, he didn't even feel any love from Claude. Fact was, he got the feeling the sooner this wedding was over, the better. Brazil, no matter how harsh, would be better.

The wedding day came, Danny was nervous. Loraine looked beautiful. Maybe Clara was right, no one could have done it better. The flowing white wedding dress, the veil, the sanctity of the marriage vows.

For better or worse
For richer or poorer....
Love, honor, obey and cherish each other.
Let no man put asunder
Till death do you part
I pronounce you man and wife
You may kiss the bride.

Danny listened to the vows, he knew he was marrying the right person. He thanked God for bringing her into his life. He knew he would love her, honor her, obey her, cherish her. And most of all, he knew he would love her until death parted them. Danny lifted the veil, her dark features, hair and eyes, only brought out her natural beauty contrasting against the white gown and veil. She was the most beautiful thing Danny had ever seen. His soul mate, his wife.

Danny softly kissed his bride.

There were tears in Danny's eyes as they turned to leave, there on the front pew were Claude, Clara, Bobbie, Modeena, and Charles. Danny looked through his tears; Claude, resolute, quite bored with the whole process. Clara, gleaming, admiring her shopping skills. Bobbie wanted a coke and to be with his friends. Modeena was crying like a baby. Danny stopped, pressed Loraine's hand and said, "Wait a minute, please." Danny walked to Modeena, tears flowing from their eyes.

Modeena said, "Danny, you is a muracle, you always has been. Yo' know you is my baby."

Danny hugged Modeena and wept, "Modeena, I love you."

Danny and Loraine entered Modeena's stretch Lincoln, Charles drove them to Modeena's private jet. Within an hour after the marriage they were on their way to Rio de Janerio.

CHAPTER THIRTY FIVE

Federico had sold his two Stearman crop dusters and returned to Brazil. He had not seen his wife and daughters in two years. The sale of his planes and the money he had earned would enable his family to live very well. He was looking forward to reuniting with Danny and Loraine as he and his family waited for the Lear jet to arrive. He wanted Danny to meet his wife and other daughters.

Danny could not resist the temptation to take the right seat, the co pilot had no problem with it, crashing into one of the plush cabin seats. The pilot walked Danny through the maze of gadgets, explaining thoroughly what function each played. It was mind boggling, yet very interesting to Danny, he thought maybe he could do this.

The money Danny and Loraine had saved was substantial, about a hundred and fifty thousand. Their plan was to rent a modest house or apartment, and get Danny his twin engine rating. Maybe a jet rating later after he was working.

The families reunited, it was a happy and joyous time. Loraine was ecstatic , she hadn't seen her mother and sisters in two years and three months. In one month she would be twenty years old. A very belated marriage in Brazil. Her younger sister Rosa was sixteen and would marry soon.

It was decided all would stay, for the time being, with Federico and family. The adobe style house was far above Brazilian standards. Its high ceiling and open windows made the heat bearable. Danny and Loraine had their own bedroom, Rosa made the sacrifice and returned to her sister's room. They knew a house or apartment would need to be found fast, but a job was the priority. Otherwise their savings and hope for the twin engine training would dwindle.

A week passed, Federico knew people in the aviation industry. All the airlines demanded two thousand hours jet time minimum. There were a few cargo twin jobs, but they wanted high hour men too. Danny was getting known around the airport, found an experienced twin trainer Federico had recommended. He was on his third lesson and picking up things easily. In a month or so he would have the multi engine license. Then what? Zero time.

With no job prospects, they decided to stay on with Federico kicking in some cash for food and utilities. Danny worked hard at his training, finishing and passing the test in four weeks. Federico's flying buddies were asked to keep their ears open if they heard of anything coming up. Months passed, Danny had applied at every available opening. He was always told he needed time, hours flown or forget it.

Out of desperation he called home, asking Clara to write to Marie. He needed the job even if it was minimum pay, he had to build some hours. Two weeks passed, he now needed out of Federico's way. The cramped quarters were putting a strain on the entire household. The letter from Argentina finally arrived, Bob would pick them up.

Danny and Loraine waited at the airport, hoping they would recognize Bob by the photograph Marie enclosed. They wouldn't have to, the most beat up twin engine Apache Danny had ever seen pulled up right outside, a hand appeared motioning to come, came from the planes window.

Danny turned to Loraine. "Are you ready for this?"

"Are you?" questioned Loraine.

Bob, cigarette smoke billowing across his face, "You Danny and Loraine?"

"Yep. That's us."

"We'll gas up and get outta here. I'm not used to traffic like this anymore." Bob fueled with the cigarette still hanging from his lips.

Danny and Loraine held their breath. Bob motioned Danny to the pilot seat as he secured the gas cap.

Danny took the pilot in command seat, the left seat, Loraine the co-pilot, the right seat. Bob crawled in the aft passenger seat crushing out his cigarette in the overflowing ashtray. Bob gave Danny the heading, "Fly for five hours then wake me up. I haven't slept in twenty hours. Make sure you keep that heading or we won't be able to refuel." Bob pulled the bill of his ball cap over his eyes, in seconds he was sound asleep.

Danny did as instructed keeping a close eye on the heading. Moments after take off they were above the rain forest, it was endless, hostile, menacing from a pilot's view. It was beautiful, lush green, hundreds of colorful birds glided above the canopies. Danny fiddled with the throttles trying to find the best engine RPM, therefore the most economical on fuel.

Loraine said it first, "We sure wouldn't want to have to force land down there."

"That's why we have two engines, we can fly with just one."

The husband and wife team talked pilot to pilot, no different than if total strangers. Loraine was right there was no place to land, entirely different than the south or the high plains of Texas. They flew on in awe of what some say is the most magnificent wonder of the world.

Four and a half hours passed. Loraine turned and woke Bob. He slowly came to life, rubbing his face as if in some stupor. He checked the heading. It was okay.

"You're doing fine, keep going." In seconds he was in a deep sleep again.

Danny shrugged his shoulders.

Loraine gave a little grin.

They pressed on, a large river was coming into view.

"Five hours is up." Loraine said.

"Wake him," Danny said.

"He just went back to sleep."

"Wake him," Danny said in a firm tone.

Again Bob slowly stirred, lifting his cap bill, checking the terrain below. "Take a right, follow the river for thirty minutes."

Danny did as directed, fighting the urge to go low and see the river close up.

This time Loraine waited the full thirty minutes before waking Bob.

"Bob, Bob," Loraine shook him, harder this time.

"Okay, you see that opening to the right?"

"No, I don't. Where?" Danny replied.

"Bank a little to the right," Bob said.

Danny did, the plane's nose moved. Now Danny saw it, a small open swath, running from the edge of the river and perpendicular to it. Danny saw no runway, grass or otherwise, only giant trees right and left of the opening. Shade and shadows, the whole thing looked smaller than a dark band aid.

Danny flew over, trying to check it out.

He looked back at Bob, hoping for some input.

Bob just grinned, saying nothing. Danny banked and started his approach, applying full flaps to slow and control his descent. It was like flying into a dark, unexplored cave. The twin touched down, Danny's eyes were doing the opposite of walking into a bright sun after a summer matinee movie. Almost blind Danny could only see the trees on both sides of him, he knew he was on the ground, but where? He continued to look at only what he could see, the tree tops.

Bob yelled, "Brakes!"

Danny was already applying them.

Bob yelled it twice, "Brakes! Brakes!" Danny mashed them hard, really hard. The plane settled, rocking to and fro. Danny's eyes were adjusting, now he could see the planes wings in partial sun, partial shade on both sides.

"Good job," Bob said un-phased. Danny turned the plane and taxied back to the river's edge.

There was not a soul in sight, nothing. Bob seemed fully awake for a change as they walked about like roadside park drivers.

"What now?" Danny asked.

"We wait, a boat will come with fuel." Bob declared.

An hour passed.

"Guess there are no schedules here." Loraine said, her voice and mannerisms somewhere between smug and sarcastic.

Bob addressed them both, it was easy to tell he was speaking as a pilot, an experienced, veteran captain. "There are no schedules, you do what you have to do to get where you're going. There are no easy landings, all are risky, most down right treacherous. There are no gas stations. There are no maintenance hangars. There are no mistakes. There are no second chances."

A boat appeared in the muddy swift current, upstream about a hundred yards out.

"Ah, the fuel," Bob said as he dug into the cargo door dragging out three army surplus C rations, tossing them like hot potatoes.

"Lunch time, I think there are some hot Cokes in there," Bob said.

They ate, drank the portions of Coke that hadn't spewed out. The rain forest was strangely quiet. Similar to a buzzing, crowded room and the arrival of the guest speaker. Then the quiet gave way to a cacophony of jungle sounds. The forest was a living, breathing, magical thing.

Danny took both engines full and began his rollout. The river looked very close, the towering trees on either side, even closer. The little twin had strength clearing and climbing.

"You got it," Bob said giving Danny another heading and adding "We should be there about this time tomorrow."

Twenty four hours later Danny circled the orphanage, checking the runway. There were five grass thatched roofs and children gathering as if to greet Santa. Danny was impressed by the ruggedness of the plane, taking every teeth chattering jar, bounding down the lumpy make shift landing strip.

Marie was there, and a hoard of children. Two other adults stood alongside her.

At last they had arrived. Danny asked Bob to sign his log book, after all, the sole purpose of being here was to build hours. Bob smiled as if he knew something Danny didn't. Danny looked puzzled, did Bob know? He signed the log book with the hint of a smirk saying nothing.

CHAPTER THIRTY SIX

Dog tired, Danny and Loraine met briefly with Marie. The two Argentine adults were introduced, Danny's body and mind were exhausted, he paid little attention to their names. Asking only for a place to sleep; Loraine was spent and as tired as Danny. They slept the remainder of the day and all night.

The sun woke Danny first, he walked to the door of the mud hut gazing out on the open fields. The huts were located in a grove of trees, the weather was good, this was not the rain forest. Danny realized they had flown beyond it, but not far.

Loraine joined Danny, they were to meet Marie and the others for breakfast.

They knew nothing of her many Blood Mary mornings, and her not so lucid past. The largest of the buildings had a string of children stair-stepped in size from smallest to largest in a line outside. Some of the little ones clung to each other in pairs, obviously they had been arranged in this fashion. Marie stood at the door, half doorman, half mother, as each one passed she spoke to them and gave them hugs. It was apparent she loved each of them.

The pair approached Marie, she abandoned her post, leading them inside and seating each separately at the head of long tables that stretched from one end of the building to the other. Danny estimated there were seats for thirty, so two or maybe three passes would need to be made to get all the children through for breakfast. All the tables had an older child placed between two younger ones, their duties were to tend to the younger ones. It was working well; pouring milk on the oatmeal, peeling bananas, some needed help eating and drinking. Spills were common, no one panicked simply going to the end of the table and getting towels and a mop bucket. The older children seemed attentive to the others, Danny wondered if they were brothers or sisters.

Danny had glanced occasionally over to Loraine, giving her a "What have I gotten myself into" look. He glanced again, her chair was empty, she had gone to assist in a big spill. One of the large pitchers of milk had shattered, she was holding her hands up, speaking in Spanish. Then English, "Stop, stop, don't stand up, you will step on the sharp glass." The maternal instincts, and being the oldest of three girls kicked in; directing, comforting, cleaning, praising the older ones that had joined in her efforts. Danny sat watching, he felt a deeper love for her, a respect; he couldn't put his finger on it, it was definitely a good feeling. Danny rose and naturally offered his help. Loraine looked at him, they were hooked the very first day. This would be their family, their life's work, their purpose.

Danny was an only child for eight years. Modeena had not spoiled him, well maybe a little. The silence of the new guests was wearing off, the place seemed louder, more complex, children streaming past on their way to other duties.

He was helping Loraine as best he could, more in the way than helping. Loraine gave him "the look", lead, follow, or get out of the way without saying a word. It was the first of many, in what was to become a long, happy, wonderful marriage.

Marie was nearing eighty years old, she got around okay, sometimes she just got so tired she had to rest. Danny could see it, inevitable someone would have to take her place. Bob ate nitro tablets like M & M's, the heart attack was looming. Everyone, including Bob knew it.

A year passed, a rigid, almost military existence. Yet it was possibly the best year either Danny or Loraine had lived. They had favorites, trying not to show it.

There were children with health problems, vaccinations to give, always a cut or bruise. None had ever seen a dentist, the solution was plenty of milk. Danny oversaw and helped with the milking, every morning and evening. Five cows, and ten milking goats, the older boys milked the cows, the girls milked the goats.

Measles, mumps, chicken pox, would send Danny on rare occasions for a doctor. Mostly the children just got over it. They were well fed, healthy and happy for the most part. The most difficult thing Danny and Loraine found was when it was time for a child to leave. Especially if they had been a favorite of one of the two, each had their own. Danny would fly them to San Palo, give them fifty dollars, and take them on job interviews. The rule was no one would be left on the streets. A job, any job, would do. The streets of San Palo were rough, plenty of trouble was around.

The children had above normal skills, bilingual in English and Spanish, good basic reading writing and arithmetic. Danny taught the more promising Algebra, geometry and trigonometry. Loraine taught language, reading, literature. All were schooled in Bible studies, said nightly prayers, and attended the frequent church services.

To Danny's dismay, no one had showed an interest in flying. It wouldn't have been possible anyway. Fuel was short, money was getting shorter, the plane's engines needed overhauling. He missed flying himself, Bob had only signed his log book the one time. Danny had figured out the altitude of flying worsened Bob's heart condition, he hadn't traveled with him much at all.

Five years passed, Bob died in his sleep three years ago. Danny and some older boys dug his grave and placed a marker. Marie could hardly get around, her movements stiff and rigid. Yet she made her way up the hill, by a small stand of trees to visit Bob's grave every day.

Danny and Loraine often watched, looking at each other, knowing someday they would depart. Loraine would rub Danny's forearm, he would look at her as if it was his last chance to ever do so. It was a long, lasting, sacred, forever kind of love.

CHAPTER THIRTY SEVEN

Loraine awoke, it was three AM; she was sick to her stomach. She wanted to through up, but couldn't. Strangely she had felt that way a week or more. Maybe she was pregnant, probably not, she hadn't had her period. That was not unusual for her, she never was very regular. Sometimes she would go two or three months.

Loraine crawled back into bed, trying not to waken Danny.

"Are you sick?" Danny mumbled.

"No, I'm alright" Loraine lied. Knowing something was not right.

That morning at breakfast Danny decided to sit at Loraine's table. He was worried about her, she hadn't been herself in awhile.

"Can I get you anything?" Danny asked.

"Yeah, I want some bacon and eggs, I'm tired of this damn oatmeal." Loraine's voice carried, she was speaking louder than normal.

A hush fell among the chattering tables, all eyes were on Loraine. Silent as a tomb, not a spoon rose. At once, Loraine began to cry, she hurriedly left. Danny sat in disbelief, he had never seen her act that way, that was not his Loraine. Something was terribly wrong.

Danny hastily told the children to continue with their meal, and chased after Loraine. He entered the mud hut, she was lying across the bed sobbing.

"I'm sorry. I don't know what came over me," Loraine was remorseful, apologetic, blubbering between words.

Danny was dumb-founded. He sat on the side of the bed in silence.

Loraine began to talk more.

"I'm tired of this goddamn place. I'm a slave, they're killing me. I'm sick of living in a house with a dirt floor, there's gotta be more to life than this. I told you I want some goddamn bacon and eggs."

Danny couldn't believe what he was witnessing, his sweet, loving wife transformed into a ranting bitch.

He stormed out, hurt, angry. Danny started the plane and took off. He did not return until the next day, no one knew where he had been.

The worn out Apache bounced down the lumpy strip. As was the custom, children surrounded as soon as the props stopped turning.

"Help me unload," Danny said.

The entire cabin was full of crated up chickens, probably ten to a cage. There were at least twelve cages. The children carried them to some nearby trees to get them out of the heat.

Danny went to the cargo hole, squealing and grunting sounds emerged. One large pig and two more crates of very small piglets had made the trip.

The children were wild, gathering closer to see, it was pandemonium. Danny was sweating profusely, covered with chicken feathers. He went to the co-pilot seat and unfastened the belt. Gingerly he removed a large crate of eggs.

Danny headed straight for the kitchen. The children followed in an unruly herd.

"Fernando, go to the plane. In the floor there is an ice chest, bring it to me please." Danny asked his most reliable elder.

Loraine came in the kitchen, flushed from her room by all the excitement.

"Where have you been?"

"Shopping," Danny replied, not trying to hid his unhappiness and anger.

Danny took a large frying pan and started the propane stove. Within minutes he had scrambled a huge mound of eggs. Loraine looked on, arms crossed, saying nothing.

Fernando came with the large cooler another older boy helped him since it was so heavy. The children gathered around the windows and the entry, they all wanted to see. None would dare enter.

Danny began to unload the giant cooler, most of the ice now water. "Have a coke," Danny popped the top handing it to Loraine. She looked at the red can in a distant way, as if saying hello to a long lost friend. Danny popped one for himself and took a long sip savoring the moment.

"Ah, nectar of the gods" Danny said still hanging on to the sarcasm. Danny began to unload the cooler, chocolate bars, cokes, beer, all sort of rare items, mascara, make-up, six Zero bars, and at the very bottom, four packages of thick sliced bacon.

Danny opened the package and began to fry the whole package. He lit another burner and started to heat another skillet.

Loraine grabbed the chocolate and drank the coke.

Danny reached in the cooler and popped a can of beer. He guzzled it down in one tilt of his head.

Loraine downed what was left of the coke Danny had opened. The bacon was sizzling. Danny flipped it over, reaching for another can of beer.

"Get two plates, please," Danny said to Loraine.

He heaped on a pile of eggs, six at least. A half a skillet of bacon on each plate.

They did not look at each other. They ate, and ate, the misery was wonderful. Danny finally spoke as he produced a small package from his pocket.

"I was thinking when I left, you either have a brain tumor or you're pregnant."

He handed her the package, it read Self Pregnancy test. Loraine smiled. God how Danny loved her.

Within an hour Loraine had the test results, it was not a brain tumor.

"We're going to have a baby," Loraine was bubbly, downright giddy.

Danny said, "That's wonderful," thinking was it? Loraine would not raise their child here, what would happen to the children.

Three months passed, Loraine's hormones were leveling off, so was the morning sickness. A twinge of both was not unusual.

Danny had been busy, building pens, he was getting a few eggs, the piglets had grown, the large one was in the new smoke house. Loraine would get her bacon and eggs. The cokes, beer and candy bars were history. It was time for another run. Danny had a growing concern about the engines, they were way past overhaul hours. He would go anyway. He had to go, Loraine needed vitamins.

The trip was six hours each way. Danny was extra careful on his pre flight, checking everything twice. He stowed away extra engine oil, he would check it once he got there.

Danny strapped in and began to start the engines, the left one started right up. The right failed to start, he tried it again. Still nothing, he shut down the left engine and walked around to the right removing the cowling and searching for the trouble. He cleaned the fuel filter, he had done that just yesterday. It was still partially clogged. He hoped he hadn't gotten hold of some bad fuel.

He strapped in again, this time both engines started. He checked every gauge carefully, the right engine twice. He took off and headed to the land of nectar, beer and chocolate.

For three hours the Apache hummed along, then the right engine started running rough. Danny went through the engine out procedures in his mind. Luckily the engine held up, the fuel filter was clogged when Danny checked it out after he landed. The plane was beginning to make him nervous, it was a good reliable plane, he knew it was far past the hours flown for an overhaul.

Marie's money was there for the children, she had seen to that for years to come. Danny had asked her about overhauling the engines. She said Bob always ran them past the allotted hours, that it was an American thing designed to make money for the mechanics and general aviation.

When he returned he would insist on the engine overhauls, if he could make it home and back.

Danny bought the goods for the orphanage, Loraine had some strange cravings, she always liked chocolate and cokes, the latest request was for tamales and dill pickles. The main thing was the pre-natal vitamins.

Danny arrived back at the plane and loaded the cargo hole and back where the seats used to be. He removed them after hauling the chickens, the seats were ruined any way. He checked that right engine one more time, the fuel filter was clear. Danny refueled and took off. The engine gave him no trouble on the way home. He thought maybe he had gotten some bad fuel, the engine did better after he refueled.

Loraine met him when he landed, she hugged him and held him longer than she normally did.

"What's wrong," Danny asked.

"I don't know, I just had a bad feeling, did the plane do alright?"

"Yeah, no problems," Danny lied not wanting to worry her. He knew she knew the state of the engines.

Danny went looking for Marie, he found her standing at the doorway, getting kids inside for the evening meal.

"I can't fly that thing one more trip without an overhaul," Danny demanded.

"Ok, take it, get it done," Marie stated without hesitation.

Danny was amused, her attitude a complete reversal. He shook his head and returned to the plane to unload. He was dragging the last items out where the seats and carpeting used to be. There was a loose screw in the flooring, it looked strange and out of place. Danny's first impulse was to go to his tool box and tighten it up. He made it to the tool box and stopped when he picked up the screwdriver. Something, he didn't know what, was not right about the screw. When he returned, he looked closely, discovering three more screws, one in each corner of the area where the backseats had once been. Danny removed the remaining screws, the floor area was now loose. He jimmied it a bit to and fore. The entire floor lifted out, it was cumbersome and could not be removed from the plane, the doors were too small for it to fit through. It was not designed to be removed. Danny looked at the secret compartment. Why would that be there he theorized? That certainly didn't come from the factory that way, someone had carefully designed and constructed it. He carefully replaced the cover.

That night Danny told Loraine of the false floor. Loraine's thoughts were that Bob had unknowingly bought the plane from drug dealers.

"How big is the compartment?" Loraine asked.

"Well, its from wall to wall wide, then to the back behind where the seats used to be," Danny said.

"How deep is it?"

"Not very, shallow actually, maybe five or six inches."

The two didn't have much to say, the compartment was empty, so it probably didn't matter.

Another month passed, time for another run.

This time Danny would stay until the engines were overhauled. He had been thinking about the compartment; what if someone discovered it during the overhaul? "Nay, ninety five percent of that work is done outside the cabin, the engines are removed and taken to a shop. The only need to actually be inside the plane would be after the engines are reworked, reinstalled and run up for testing. So what if they found the compartment, it's empty."

Danny tried not to let it bother him, after all he was completely innocent. He had done nothing. His imagination was taking him places he didn't want to go. Besides it was empty.

Danny was underway about two hours into the six hour trip. The auto pilot was engaged, it gave him time to think.

It's empty, no problem....his mind was working overtime. What ifs were beginning to fill his head.

What if its not empty?

What if its loaded with God knows what?

What if its drugs?

What if I'm a patsy?

"God damn," Danny released the autopilot, and started his descent to a remote isolated strip he knew.

It thirty minutes he was on the ground. Tool box out, he opened the floor compartment. "My God, my God," Danny said aloud as he looked at a packed compartment. Little white bags wrapped in plastic secured with duct tape. Danny's jaw was wide open, in momentary denial. Then he began to count the tightly bound packages, each about the size of a 13 ounce coffee sack. There were forty. Danny couldn't get one loose, they were packed so tightly.

Danny could hear a plane approaching, that's odd he thought, sometimes weeks passed without seeing a plane out here. The plane banked and made a low pass. Danny knew whoever was in that plane was protecting their investment.

He nervously fastened the lid back, The plane might land, then what? They'd kill me in a heartbeat. "I gotta get outa here," Danny spoke aloud.

He didn't see the other plane as he lifted off. He knew he couldn't hear it over his own engines. Danny didn't go high, the other plane was a new King Air, he could not out climb him, or out run him, maybe with luck he could out maneuver him.

Danny made a mad dash. Low, gray clouds sagged across the sky. He could see the rain forest. Zig-zagging, beginning the longest crop dusting run of his life. The gear was up on the Apache, if it were down it could hang a tree top.

Danny was not sure if he was being pursued or not, he didn't want to know. Evasive action was natural, he didn't think about it he just did it.

It started to rain, the wipers smeared the windshield. Blind he began to climb. No choice now. The Apache chugged up through the thick dark low clouds. Danny welcomed it, he would hide in the clouds. He had to climb, he had burned a lot of fuel zig-zagging low.

Danny broke through on top of the clouds. He immediately set his heading once at ten thousand feet, the normal cruise.

What would he do when he got there? Go to the authorities? No, not down here, they are extremely harsh on drug dealers. Get rid of it? No, wouldn't have a clue how. Let them have it? Who are they?

Danny landed, walked away from the plane, straight into the air terminal. He fumbled through his wallet and found the number.

The phone was ringing. I hope she's at home. The third ring, Danny knew her voice instantly.

"Modeena?"

Modeena listened and recalled the past, she grew angry, a little at first. Then she thought of Danny, this horrible woman could put him in prison, her anger was peaking.

"Well, Modeena know how to handle 'dis."

Danny looked relieved.

Modenna and Charles arrived the next day.

"Go git us a taxi, find the best hotel in town," she told Charles. Modeena got on the phone immediately, calling the people that sold her the Lear jet.

"Ya'll got somebody down here 'dat speaks 'dis language. I gotz ta buy me a plane". The man on the phone said they had a representative in Buenous Aries. He would be dispatched immediately. Danny interrupted Modeena.

"I don't own the plane, Marie does."

"Don't you worry, how much dat plane worth?"

"It's completely trashed, needs two new engines. Twenty thousand, tops."

"Danny, go get the plane ready, we goin' to pay a visit out to dat orphanage and cancel dat overhaul."

The Apache was right where Danny had parked it two days ago. Modeena filled the seat and then some. Danny knew he would have to depart about 1:00 AM, that would put them arriving after dawn. He had to have light to see the strip.

Danny hadn't done much night flying, it was dangerous enough in broad daylight. He pushed on, they could see the strip, dawn had broken. Danny breathed easier once on the ground, he had spent the entire trip worrying about the engines. Where he would land without being able to see the ground. He knew the answer, you didn't.

Modeena told Danny to stay with the plane and she went straight to Marie. Marie was directing the lines at breakfast, she was always the first to arrive.

Marie could tell by the look on Modeena's face, it was not going to be a pleasant surprise. Marie spoke first, trying to avoid conflict in front of the children.

"I see you're upset, let's go to my room to talk.:

"We ain't goin' no wheres, we talkin' now!" Modeena's blood pressure was surging.

"What about 'dat white powder in 'dat plane? Is you pullin dat same shit you did wiff Mr. Claude?"

"What on earth are you talking about Modeena?" Either Marie

was playing dumb, knowing her hand was stuck in the cookie jar or maybe she really didn't know.

"Bull shit, you know zackly what I'm talkin about!" Modeena was not to be fooled by Marie's play acting.

"How much you want fer dat plane?"

Marie stammered, "It's not for sale."

"I said, how much do you want fer dat plane? I'm buying it or I'm crashing it."

A look of total panic came over Marie. Modeena had her in checkmate, knowing she would follow through.

Marie hesitantly said, "$800,000."

Modeena looked Marie right in the eyes. "Mr. Danny done tol me, dat plane be worff only $20,000. Now why Modeena gonna pay $800,000?"

Marie knew she was caught, so she started another trail of lies and deceit. "Well, I'll have to get another pilot, and new engines, maybe even a new plane. You could consider it a gift to the orphanage, take it off your taxes."

"I done wrote you one check and Mr. Danny ended up down here'a anyway. I'm writin' you a check for twenty thousand, we be leavin' your cargo on the ground right here."

Loraine showed up, watching the encounter a few yards away. It was too heated to say a word. Modeena turned to Loraine.

"Don't pack nothin', go tell Danny to refuel the plane and unload the cargo. We leavin' here right now."

Loraine backed up cautiously, then broke into a run toward the strip. Danny had already refueled knowing he would take Modeena back. Loraine and Danny feverishly started unloading the powder.

Ten minutes passed, Danny began to worry, Modenna wrote the check for the plane when he told her how much it was worth. "She should be back by now," Danny said.

"You know how long it takes her to walk. Give her five more minutes," Loraine answered.

"I'm so confused about all this, I thought Marie was a born again Christian. That we were doing God's work here."

"I know, that's what I thought too" Loraine said pausing, wondering how doing something good had become something evil.

Another ten minutes passed, Danny knew something had gone wrong. He couldn't, he wouldn't leave her.

Danny leaped from the plane, engines running.

"Hold it here," he yelled at Loraine, "I'll be back."

Danny dashed up the slight hill back toward the buildings. He could see a crowd of children encircling someone on the ground. Danny ran faster, breaking through the children.

Modeena was on the ground, she was breathing, the color returning to her pale brown face.

"Back up, back up, give her some air," Danny yelled.

She was coming around. "Are you alright Modeena?" Danny questioned.

"Yeah, blood pressure," was all she could manage.

"Can you make it to the plane?"

"Give me a minute."

Five minutes later, Danny waited,, "Where is Marie?" he asked the children.

They pointed to her room.

"Where are all the big kids?"

They pointed to Marie's room.

Modeena was on her feet now, slowly they made their way toward the strip. It seemed forever, Modeena had to stop and rest. Twenty minutes later Danny was trying to shut the plane's door. Modeena seemed bigger now that Danny was trying to manhandle her.

Danny jumped in where the back seats used to be. Loraine rolled out and pulled up, they were on their way.

No surprise, the right engine was running rough. Danny told her to watch the manifold pressure, they had a long trip ahead of them. Modeena was killing them with cigarette smoke, she was on her third one since takeoff. Air born only thirty minutes, they begged Modeena to put it out, she ignored them saying, "Crack 'dat window, it'll suck all dis smoke outa hear."

One of the planes instruments contained a chronograph, a timer to tell how many minutes had elapsed since take off. Modeena watched it intently, 32 minutes, 33 minutes, 34 minutes.

Danny sat with his back to the aft bulkhead watching Modeena, trying to figure out what the hell she was doing. She seemed extraordinarily nervous.

Thirty five minutes to the second Modeena said, "I gotz to pee."

"Loraine, hit that emergency strip, it's straight ahead about five minutes, just start your descent. You should have plenty of time," Danny told Loraine, shouting over the engine noise. It was much louder now that the seats, carpeting, and part of the fabric on the rear side walls were gone.

Loraine made a good landing on the grass, not a runway at all. Just a smooth spot in an open field, Danny had used it for pee stops, and just to stretch his legs. There was a grove of trees nearby, shade from the sun, maybe Modeena would smoke there. Everyone, including Modeena, needed some fresh air.

They unloaded themselves, and walked the short distance to the trees. Danny had never seen her so nervous.

"What's bothering you Modeena, we got away didn't we?" Danny said.

"No, we didn't," Modeena said with the emphasis on "we."

"What do you mean "we" didn't?" Danny asked.

"The authorities know about 'dis operation, they is paid off."

"How do you know that?" Danny said, half jokingly.

"Cause Marie done told me."

"Well, we will just wait until we get back to the states and go to the FBI, they have units that specialize in drug enforcement."

"How you know 'dat they ain't paid off?"

"Because things are different there, they're honest, trustworthy."

"Dat so? Let me see all of South and Central America, and Mexico is dishonest and the good ole USA ain't?"

"That's right, Modeena." Danny said in a boasting tone.

"Child you ain't gotz sense enough to get out ta rain. All 'dis corruption, and all 'dis money, just gonna run up to the border and stop dead in its tracks?"

"That's right Modeena. We have a democracy, a Bill of Rights, a Constitution that protects its citizens....I thought you needed to pee?"

Modeena ambled down to the trees.

Danny and Loraine sat next to each other on the ground half

lying down. Danny put his hand on the small pooch just below her navel. They smiled and kissed, looking deeply into each other's eyes. They continued to touch each other in consoling, loving ways. Knowing they had to go to the authorities, and tell what they knew. Was Marie involved? It was not a definite. Danny thought probably, then maybe not. It angered him to think it possible.

Modenna made it back. "I didn't want to tell ya'll 'dis, but my chest is really hurtin."

Danny jumped to his feet and hurriedly loaded his passengers. Once in the air he reached in Modeena's purse. Found the Salems and started throwing them one by one out the window.

Danny felt in the purse for more, fumbling, still trying to fly the plane. His hand felt something cold, something steel. He placed the plane on autopilot even though he was still climbing. Danny grabbed the purse and inspected its contents closely, it was a gun. A big bulky hell of a gun.

"Why do you have this?" Danny yelled as if he had caught a child with it.

"Marie's done ordered me to shoot you both."

"Are you crazy? You're talking out of your head."

Danny turned to Loraine who was now in the back. "Maybe she's had a stroke.:"

"I ain't had no stroke. I knows what Marie do, I ain't made all dat money on no market. I been sellin' and pushin' dope since you was eight or nine years old."

A look of shock came over Danny, he was stone silent. Modeena was sobbing. "But I can't be killin' nobody, especially you. I loves you, you know I do."

Modeena had worked herself into a remorseful, blubbering state, tears flowing. The years of lies and deceit were being revealed.

Danny finally spoke, "How did you ever get mixed up with her?"

"They come to the house years ago, Mr. Claude done went kinda crazy. He be lookin' outa the windows all hours of da day, not sleepin' at night. I knowed somethin'weren't right. Then dees two men start start follin' me home, I learnt den Mr. Claude be havin' dope in hisin car tires. Mr. Claude have nothin to do wiff it. But Miss Clara she be knowin' all about it. Din Miss Clara start givin' me money, lots of money. I knowed I was gonna haff to do something for it, dat's when I learnt theys puttin' 'dat dope in dem cotton bales at the compress. Lord I knows it was wrong, I jest ain't never had dat much money and the mo' I gotz the mo' I wanted. Miss Clara, she tell me everything to do, I takes my orders from her."

"And Marie told you to kill us?" Danny asked.

"Oh we wees dead right now, if'in I didn't shoot ya, she be shootin' me and you."

"Good God Modeena, you were gonna shoot us?

"No, honey chil', I told Marie I would sos we can get away, but there ain't no gettin' away. Everybody includin' me know 'dat. Yea, I thought about shootin' you so you never knows about all 'dis and you wouldn't know yous about to be kilt."

"I see, kind of a mercy killing," Danny said smugly, not quite sure she hadn't had a stroke.

Modeena picked up on his doubts instantly, "A helicopter pos' ta come pick me up after I shoot ya, they bes coming for us."

Danny arched his brow, then his eyes narrowed, taking a long look at Modeena, "You ain't lying?"

"No chil' I ain't lying."

Modeena, that's a fantastic story.

"You're sure your not lying?"

"No chil'" tears streaming.

Danny could tell she was telling the truth. "Is there anything else you haven't told me?"

"Lord yeah, theys lots mo'!"

Danny closed his eyes in a silent mini prayer. Finally he managed a "What?"

"Charles he ain't my man."

"You mean he's not your boyfriend?"

"Yeah, dat's right. He be a FBI man."

Danny turned and looked at Loraine. "She's had a stroke."

"I ain't had no Gaud damn stroke! I bees tellin' da truff!"

"Then why doesn't he arrest Marie and you?"

"Cause he ain't no good FBI man, he be knowin' all about drug dealin'. He done told me if they wanted to keep all the drugs outta da country, they could do it, shut it all down in a week. Dem is the big money peoples, theys all senators and congressmen, lawyers, judges, even the police."

"Holy shit Modenna, you telling me the entire United States is corrupt?"

"No chil', it be the whole world."

Danny squinted into the sun, "don't you think thats a little far fetched, everyone can't be bad, on the take."

"Naw, it ain't far fetched, the people with the real power, dey control it all. Who live, who die, who make money, who don't."

"Then why are there so many arrests for drug dealers and users?"

"Cause dey da customers, da little mens; Charles done told me deys arrest dem cause lawyers and courts make millions of dollars off 'em."

"Really," Danny replied half scoffing.

"Dat so, when dey puts 'em in jail, dey ain't stayin' long. Dey gets early release so's dey can do it all again, only dey learn to be better at it in jail."

Modeena, Modeena....Danny was going to start a sermon, but he spotted a helipcopter about two thousand feet below.

His mind raced, he had never seen a helicopter all the time he had flown rural Argentina. They were only around the big cities. Danny was catching on slowly, hauntingly slow. The real world just slapped Danny De Moss right in the face.

CHAPTER THIRTY EIGHT

Danny desperately tried to evade the chopper. It was low and slow, soon he would be past them within view. Danny frantically switched the autopilot off, feathering both engines. He looked around for a cloud. Anywhere to hide, there were none. Still too fast to make a turn without shooting out in front of the chopper. Only one choice remained. Danny pulled hard on the yoke. The Apache's nose pointed straight up. An engine off stall maneuver was his only option. The plane seemed to climb forever, finally it began to shudder and vibrate, then the stall alarm sounded drowning any other sounds and thoughts. Danny knew he would need to regain control as the plane started slipping backward tail first toward the earth. Everything loose in the cockpit, maps, Modeena's purse, Loraine, were temporarily suspended in mid air.

Danny yelled, "Hold on!" He could feel Loraine's feet pressing against the back of his seat. The nose was pointing straight down hurtling at high speed. If Danny couldn't control the dive and fast the plane would break up in mid air. He pulled hard on the yoke and lifted his feet off the rudder pedals. A diving spin could prove fatal. The wings were level, the nose slowly rose. Danny pulled it off. The chopper was still out in front, they had not been detected.

"Good Gaud!" Modeena exclaimed holding both hands over her chest. Danny was sweating, his hands still clammy, not accustomed to being out of control in an airplane, even if it was temporary and deliberate.

"Now what?" Danny asked.

"They ain't gonna be no gettin' away. Ain't no place in 'dis world to hide. Ain't no place in 'dis world to go dat deys can't find us." Modeena's negativity was totally out of character, alarming to Danny.

Loraine had the answer, "Remember where we refueled on the river? Do we have enough fuel to get there?"

"It'll be close. Nightfall is more important than the fuel." Danny turned toward the river flying blind, dead reckoning. The sunset was brilliant hues of crimson when the trio landed. The right engine gulped fuel. They would be stranded until the river boat arrived. Tonight would be hungry and sleepless. A plan, any plan, to get away, to survive.

The boat did not come the following day, Danny found a spring fed stream. At least they had fresh water. Modeena was down to her last Salem, panic was setting in. Danny used Modeena's gun to hunt. He was cautious, using only one bullet on a wild hog.

On the third day Danny examined the right engine. It was leaking oil, the fuel didn't matter now, the plane was done.

A boat came down the river on the fourth day. They all boarded, not knowing where they were going. A feeling of helplessness was overpowering. The native boy guided the boat expertly, stopping at several small villages. The people were hospitable, giving them fish and yams. Modeena even managed to roll a bummed cigarette. She drew on it like it was her last. Adoring the smoke as it waffled before her eyes.

Loraine and Danny had been praying as they always did. This time Danny added quotes from Jesus in John 7 Verse 6, Jesus said to them, my time has not come, but your time is always here. The world cannot hate you, but it hates me because I testify of it that its works are evil." The native boy, Raul, listened to their prayers, which always included the Lord's Prayer. Raul remained silent as he watched them pray and their faith grow. He knew they were in big trouble, Danny always kept his eyes moving. Raul knew the look of a stalked animal.

Loraine prayed the rosary each morning and each night. When she wasn't praying she nervously fumbled the rosary beads.

Sometimes she would stare at the crucifix, it was hauntingly sublime. In her heart Loraine knew God would see them through, yet she wondered had her time come.

Raul had a crude homemade tatoo of a cross on his upper arm. Loraine had noticed it when Raul would let the boat drift to gig fish. It was obvious he knew the river well, he was known in every village and received with open enthusiasm. Passengers were not his usual cargo, fuel of some type or another gas, kerosene, batteries and bundles of sulfur matches lined the hull. A small outboard motor was used to go up river to the supply drop. Now he drifted with the current, learning from Loraine their plight. They spoke in Spanish, Danny on occasion would give Loraine "the look". She knew what it meant. Could he be trusted? Their lives hanging in the balance of a twenty year old native boy.

A village popped into view, Raul announced it was the end of his journey, he would be returning up river. There was a make shift floating pier made of old gasoline drums. Children frolicked in the water, the adults gathered. As they grew closer Loraine could see a priest standing just short of the pier. Loraine looked at Raul. In Spanish Raul said, "May God be with you all, go with Father he will get you to the right people."

CHAPTER THIRTY NINE

Father Lucas Dorn stood at the foot of the pier. An Irish Catholic priest exiled to South America after a run in with a radical feminist nun. At least she was in his opinion, the argument was abortion and a woman's right to choose. Father Dorn was adamant, murder was not a choice, even if the mother's life hung in the balance, God's will would prevail.

Loraine, Danny and Modeena approached, shook hands and Danny started to explain. Father Dorn interrupted, "I have information from Father Prentice," the sometimes priest at the orphanage. Danny asked, "What did he tell you?"

"He said you were in trouble. Drug lords chasing you; to kill you. Somehow you were unknowingly smuggling drugs. That Loraine was a devout Catholic and you were on your way to finding the same peace and faith. On the other hand, I may have some distressing news for you. He said the large black woman was the reason for the trouble. The authorities are looking for her and your plane. They intend to kill you all."

"The authorities?" Danny asked.

"No, the drug cartel," Father Dorn replied.

"Oh, can I trust the authorities?" Danny quipped back.

"I know of one man, he's a member of my church. He can be trusted, but there's a catch."

"What's that?"

"Modenna will have to give herself up." Father Dorn's tone

saddened, somehow he knew Danny's connection to Modenna. Possibly he had spoken with Marie, Danny thought. Mistrust and a nervous twitch in his stomach hardened Danny's attitude toward Father Dorn. "I can't trust him," he thought, his eyes darting and shifting, he could feel his pulse in his temple. Danny couldn't describe the feeling, he hated it. Logic and the look Loraine was giving him, temporarily lifted his panic and dismay. Danny knew he couldn't and wouldn't turn Modeena over to the Argentina police. They would throw her in one of their infamous prisons, urine running down the walls, only enough food to survive; hostile, disgustingly violent guards and inmates. A hell on earth, a valley of tears and torment.

"Hell no," Danny shouted.

Father Dorn looked puzzled, Danny's reply was too late, awkward.

"No what, my son?" Father Dorn retorted.

"I can't give her up to them, she's like a mother to me. Fact is, she is my mother."

Father Dorn looked over the frame of his horn rim spectacles in disbelief.

"She raised me from a baby after my mother died," Danny shouted, trying to explain his deepest feelings.

Father Dorn approached Danny and embraced him. He could feel his pain, frustration, and anguish. Danny broke down and began to cry. Loraine looked on, wanting to hold and comfort him.

In a while Father Dorn, slapped Danny on the back. A clear signal that the emotional release had reached the appropriate limit. "Pray, my son."

Modenna stood in silence. She wondered did the Father smoke? It has been a whole day, the craving was not waning, maybe it was more intense then ever. Her legs and ankles were swollen from the high blood pressure. More importantly her medication was down to her last two pills.

Father Dorn led the party down a small path that disappeared into the thick jungle. They traveled slowly, Father Dorn knew where he was going, his followers did not, and didn't ask. They simply put their trust in him, unquestioning divine trust.

After a half day of what seemed like a random maze of trails and switch backs they came to an opening. The jungle gave way to a rolling plain sprinkled with tall tress. The red clay stuck to their shoes. Everyone was tired, sweaty and hungry. Especially Loraine.

There was no food, no cigarettes, only a small container of water hung around Father Dorn's neck. He dispensed it with care, rationing only communion size portions.

Night was falling, the Father said, "We have only one hour before we reach the church. Can you continue or would you rather rest until morning?"

All agreed to forge on, not knowing what to expect once they arrived. Would there be food, water, a bed?

The reddish muck on their shoes slowed the pace. A small church appeared. It looked drab and weathered beneath it's once white exterior. In the rear there was a small living quarters.

Father Dorn said the blessing at dinner. Asking for guidance and direction, ending the prayer with the Lord's prayer and several Hail Mary's. Modeena looked a bit confused, the church and the Catholic religion seemed strange and a world away from the black Mississippi Delta.

Father Dorn bedded them down in the sanctuary on bed rolls, the blankets felt comforting. Loraine was full of Father Dorn's stew and asleep in less than a minute. Modeena was tired, the journey hardest on her, she didn't even want a cigarette. She was asleep on her feet. Danny tossed and turned all night, he watched Loraine sleep, thinking how lucky he was and how much he loved her. He looked at the crucifix and the eucharest and said his prayers, sleep overtook his thoughts at last.

Father Dorn aroused the group before daylight. They were on the move back toward the river, backtracking over yesterday's footprints. Danny questioned, "Father, this is where we were yesterday. Where are we going?"

"We went to the church for two reasons; one for food and lodging; second to confirm we were not followed. We were not followed," the Father added.

"What's the plan Father?"

"Trust me, I can't tell you, others would be endangered if you knew that."

Danny asked no more questions, the day's journey wore on into the afternoon and the jungle. Half way through the Father took a turn in the jungle, down river. Night was approaching as they met with the river. The air was thick with mosquitoes as the dusky hue hung between night and day. Two large trees had been felled into the water, the current pushing and holding them at a 45 degree angle to shore.

Suddenly the jungle sounds erupted into a load roar, then a second. Danny recognized the sound instantly, so did Loraine. Aircraft engines firing up, and now doing a run up. Warming up for take off. A bright light shown on the river. They could see the silhoutte of the sea plane coming down river. Father Dorn hurried them onto the downed logs. The plane, engines running, loaded the fugitives. The plane drifted slowly from the logs to the middle of the river. The pilot jammed the throttles, they were airborne and climbing in two minutes. Father Dorn made the sign of the cross, said a short prayer and disappeared into the dark jungle.

Danny could recognize the pilot from the glow of the instrument panel. It was Felipi, he was one of the older boys from the orphanage. Loraine spoke to him in Spanish. He was now 21. He left the orphanage at 16, like all the others.

"Where are we going?" Danny asked in broken Spanish.

"I take you back to Brazil, back to Federico."

"Daddy," Loraine said rolling her eyes up; her prayers had been answered.

CHAPTER FORTY

Federico met the trio on the Amazon. No one asked where the sea plane was obtained. Danny and Loraine knew Federico's connections; Modenna unaware of the complications and sacrifice.

Federico hugged his daughter as if risen from the dead.

"You look great, you're getting fatter." Federico said as he extended his arms as far as they would go without losing touch with her shoulders. He was beaming.

Just as quickly he turned to Danny.

"You son of a bitch, you drag my daughter off to who the hell knows where, and get tripped up in some drug smuggling shit."

In Federico's ire flames of anger shot from his eyes, "You son of a bitch, son of a bitch."

Danny was trying to talk, but Federico wouldn't let him.

"Daddy, Daddy," calming him somewhat. "It wasn't Danny's fault, he didn't know the plane had a secret compartment. We found it by accident."

"Bullshit, I warned this gringo when I was training him. Know your aircraft, know your cargo, weight distribution alone should have told him. You have to be part of the plane."

Danny and Loraine knew Federico's tempter. The only thing they could do was to take the ass chewing. Soon he would punch himself out, run out of words.

"Come on. God dammit, let's go before we're spotted."

They hurriedly switched planes, Danny shoved the pontoons of both planes from the bank, hopping on and taking the right seat.

Federico was cooling somewhat.

"You ever fly one of these?"

"No," Danny said knowing few or no words was best.

"Take her my friend, just watch the current for stick ups or loose logs."

"Altimeter setting, altitude, heading." Danny asked in his best professional manner.

Fernando gave him the information but not without a little kick. "Well at least I taught your dumb ass something."

Danny remained calm and aloof, not wanting to tangle.

They flew for hours. Modenna slept, the ordeal drained her to the point of physical and emotional exhaustion. Finally Danny said, "What's the plan?"

Federico cut his eyes sharply and jambed his thumb over his shoulder toward Modenna. The quickness of his motion said, "I don't trust her."

Danny thought after the gesture, closing his open mouth without ever saying a word. They flew on toward the ocean. Once they crossed the coastline Federico announced, "I'll take her from here."

Danny estimated they flew out about fifty miles. Then Federico started to descend, Danny could see only open choppy seas. The landing was rough and bumpy, so bumpy Loraine held her womb as if cradling the child in her arms.

"Are you alright?" Danny asked.

"Yeah," she answered. "Are you sure you have a plan?" looking fearlessly in her father's eyes.

"Yes, Yes" Federico said. "Sorry about the landing, I didn't think about the baby."

"I see, even you make mistakes?"

"Yes, Loraine, even I make mistakes."

Federico got the message, keep jacking with Danny and you'll get some of your own shit.

They drifted for over an hour. Loraine was beginning to get queasy. Then she began to vomit. The smell set off a chain reaction. All of them, even Federico, had the heaves.

A boat appeared on the horizon, but it went unnoticed during the bout of sea sickness. The boat was almost on top of them before Fernando realized it. Luckily it was the pick up boat. Danny, Loraine, and Modenna departed the smelly craft. Vomit slushing back and forth with the motion of the waves.

Federico asked the men on the boat for a bucket. They obliged, laughing and joking about the mess.

Loraine had the words, "You see Daddy, you shouldn't loose your temper. God will punish you."

The plane and the boat drifted apart. Federico running a single man bucket brigade of salt water through the craft.

Loraine could see the coastline faint and hazy on the horizon. It had been an hour since the rendevous. The sea plane passed them low, rocking its wings. Danny looked at Loraine, "I'm ready to get back to the states, I'm homesick."

"Me too, besides I want our baby to be born in America."

Federico boarded the trio for a few days. Loraine enjoyed the visit, her sisters were excited about the baby. Modenna was recuperating, two packs a day and ham sandwiches between puffs. Her happy go lucky glow was returning to her pale cheeks.

Federico, on the fourth morning, gathered them. "Here is what is going to happen. I will fly you to Venzenula near Caracas. From there you will go to Mexico by boat. Do you still have your driver's licenses?"

"Yes" all three answered.

"Good, it's all arranged. Remember, don't show your license unless you're asked."

"Where do we go in Mexico?" Danny asked.

"It's all flexible, it has to be. On the boat, a man named Paco will meet you, his job is to get you to the states. He may take you through Texas or New Mexico. He has been paid half his money, I won't pay the other until you call me from the U.S. Okay?"

"Okay," they all chimed.

The plane made good time, the touch down in Vensuela was uneventful. The landing strip was as Danny and Loraine expected, a small swath hacked out of a field of tall grass. A car approached immediately.

Loraine held her Dad's hand, tears filled his eyes. They both knew. It may be the last time they would see each other. This time Loraine was the strong one, "You're too resourceful not to come and see my baby. I love you Papa."

The car departed. Paco was at the boat waiting. The craft was small, but had a cabin and sleeping quarters. At one time the vessel would have been expensive, maybe thirty or forty years ago. Now it was drab, the white paint washed down to a dingy gray. Perfect for the job, unobtrusive, common to the eye and sea.

Each had a small bag, crammed to the brink with essentials. Toliet paper the only item too bulky not to include. Federico had warned them, "Don't trust this guy Paco. He could strand you somewhere or worse. Keep an eye on him. You know he could keep the money I already paid him. Be careful. Be really careful." Loraine was replaying her father's thoughts, almost a lecture in her head. Her eyes flashed each time they passed on the tiny cramped vessel.

Paco was young, not much older than Loraine. There was a rough texture to his dark brown unshaven face which seemed to melt into the same color as his gold teeth. The way he smiled at Loraine made her uncomfortable. He made no attempt to hide his attraction to her. A dog in heat kind of look.

Danny sensed his desires. "Stay close to me, don't let him get a chance to jump us."

"Okay, he scares me. His eyes seem distant like he's in his own world."

"Yeah, I know," Danny said.

Modenna's bag was lined with cigarettes, the entire bottom and both sides, there was little room for anything else. She had a toothbrush, some blue wasp perfume and a single change of clothes. The nicotine withdrawal still fresh in her mind.

Several tedious days later they arrived in a small fishing village. Paco secured the craft at a pier, obviously he had been there many times. Another man approached, small, dark brown, shirtless. They exchanged keys. The shirtless man boarded the vessel.

Paco said, "Come, come quickly." A car was parked nearby, the key opened the door. Modenna slowed them down, Paco sang

"Handela, handela." Modenna never switched gears, stuck in near morbid obesity. They departed down a narrow dirt road.

CHAPTER FORTY ONE

The border was near, Nueva Laredo a god forsaken filthy little slum, scattered doorless shacks made of rusted corrugated tin. The main street of commerce scattered with loose chickens and skinny mongrel dogs. They would cross at night, the U.S. guard paid to look the other way. Once across they would need to move fast, be in San Antonio by daybreak. There was safety there, at least a jump point toward home.

Danny poked coins into the pay phone. He was in a desolate, back street Spanish neighborhood. The street light whimpering rays illuminating only enough to see the holes in the rotary dial.

"Dad, it's Danny."

"Where the hell are you?"

"San Antonio, Loraine and Modenna are with me."

"Okay, what do you want me to do? Jesus Christ it's five o'clock in the morning."

"We're in trouble Dad. I'll tell you about it once I get home. Right now I need five hundred dollars to get us there."

"Tell me now. I'm awake. That's a lot of money."

"Dad, I don't have time, I need to hire someone to bring us there by car. I can't take a plane or bus."

"Why can't you, you in some kind of trouble with the law?"

Danny rested his forehead on top of the black box, the glass enclosure suddenly felt claustrophic.

He knew he would not get a dime from Claude without further explanation. He began the story with a quick nervous tempo.

"Modeena is a drug kingpin. She made her money selling cocaine—not trading commodities. Charles is an FBI agent gone bad working for the cartel. He, ugh, they are going to kill us Dad."

"Woe, woe, you're going to fast, slow down."

"Dad send the money to Paco Hernandez. Western Union Station at the airport."

"You're three minutes is up. Deposit two dollars and twenty five cents please.:"

"Dad, Dad, it's a matter of life and death, please."

The line went silent. Danny dug in his blue jean pockets knowing there was nothing to find.

Danny entered the dingy handprinted apartment door. The odor of too many people hung in the stagnant air. Carefully he stepped among the sleeping bodies on the floor seeking Loraine and Modenna. As he approached Paco appeared silhoutted in the early morning light, shirtless, two buttons on top of his jeans undone. He was looking at Loraine. The look Danny hated.

"Amigo, maybe we work a deal, hey?" The hair stood on Danny's neck, he never felt true rage. Kill the son of a bitch right now, take his money and get the hell out of here. Bad thoughts rushed through him, overtaking better judgment. Danny bowed his shoulders and made a quick step toward Paco. Paco was ready, a large knife was brandished from his hip pocket in a flash. Danny froze. No chance. Paco twisted the knife blade in the air, his gold teeth and blade glittered.

"Not today Amigo, we still have business."

"If you ever touch her, I'll kill you." Paco smiled and turned away.

Danny took his place on the floor next to Loraine. She slept unaware, Modenna never budged.

The car was switched for a windowless van. Paco drove with another Hispanic male in the passenger seat. The trio crouched in the bare cargo compartment. Paco entered the airport terminal returning in ten minutes.

"You got it?" Danny asked.

"Yeah, Amigo, I got it." Paco counted out a hundred dollars and gave it to his companion. The passengers watched helplessly as the unknown man opened his door and walked to the driver's side. Paco opened his door and stepped out. The other man took the wheel. Danny watched for Paco to come in front, to pass by the front windshield.

The new guy started the van and quickly pulled away. Danny craned his neck trying to watch the front and the back for Paco. There he was in the rear window walking away.

"Wait, stop!"

The man kept driving as Paco got in another car behind them.

Loraine started to cry. Modenna was yelling, "Stop you mother fucker, you gotz our money!"

Danny made a move to the front only to see a handgun pointing over the new driver's shoulder.

In very good English the young man said, "You want it now or later?"

Modenna screamed, "Good God he gonna kill us!" The driver turned west from the airport entrance, back toward Laredo. The captors huddled in a corner, "We have to rush him" Danny said in a low, whispering voice.

"I wouldn't try anything, if anyone moves past the rear wheels that's who I shoot first."

The young driver was confident, cocky, enjoying the sadistic rush of power.

It began to rain. Mr. X donned a pair of shooting glasses from his pocket, slipping the yellow lense and heavy metal frame on his face.

"These are great for shooting and driving in the rain." Mr. X quipped as he continued to enjoy his domination over the captors. Mr. X drove for over an hour west, then turned off on a black topped farm to market road. The rain was still coming down, harder now, a torrent of water temporarily blinding view between slaps of high speed wipers. Thunder and lightening abounded.

Mr. X stopped. Then turned left onto a gravel road.

"I haven't been here in a month or so," he laughed, spinning the drum of the revolver like a kid with a toy. "You know, I just love doing this, it's a real good job. A hundred bucks to do what I would do for free."

"Shut up, if you are going to kill us, do it!" Danny shouted.

"Okay, I'm gonna kill you alright. Do any of you want to say a little prayer before you meet your maker? I really do like to see them beg. Maybe I'm your God, think so?"

The rain was letting up. Mr. X pulled to the side and stopped.

"Get out and get on your knees." The young punk stood over them spinning the drum Russian roulette style.

"God, please forgive me fer my sins and every thang I done wrong on dis earff."

"Hail Mary, full of grace, pray for us now and at the hour of our death."

"Good night, sweet dreams," Mr. X's last taunt.

Danny could feel the man behind him extend his arm and cock the hammer. "Blam, the loudest crack, the earth trembled. Danny could feel the shock. Modeena and Loraine were screaming hysterically.

Danny was wondering why his eyes could still see. Why was he not falling face first into the coarse gravel.

Thud.

The sound was from behind. Danny turned. Mr. X was smoking, the heavy metal frame of the shooting glasses melted into his face. Every inch of his body emitted the odor of burning flesh. His bowels blown out of his rectum still sizzling like bacon.

"Good God Almighty," Modeena said. They stood motionless in an adrenaline induced paralysis. "Lightnin' done struck him dead!"

Finally Modeena said, "Danny, get the gun and our money."

Danny, shell shocked, stood in numbness, muscles twitching. Modeena gave him a shove. "Get da money, Get da gun." Danny finally moved. The money was scorched, but not badly. Danny searched for the gun but couldn't find it. He rolled Mr. X over with the heel of his boot. There was the gun, he picked it up, but dropped it quickly from the heat. They all gazed down on the very dead Mr. X, the gun barrel melted and bent, the body still smoking.

Danny showered the corpse with loose gravel making the run

back to the farm to market road. Thirty minutes passed, no one spoke.

"Go south toward Corpus Christi, we can't chance being spotted in San Antonio," Loraine said.

"Yeah, you're right," Danny managed to answer. The shock was fresh, it would last for weeks. The pale trio rode the back roads, twisting and turning, working their way east. The Louisiana state line was a welcome site, tight forced smiles, then onward into the night.

Danny pulled over around three in the morning, a side road off the rural highway they were tracking. They slept the exhaustion off in a couple of hours, then continued on toward Mississippi. The adrenaline hangover causing uncontrolled spasmodic twitching."

"I'm hungry Danny." "Me too," Modeena clamored.

Danny seemed to take the events hardest. He felt responsible for them all. The pressure never let up. Food was far from his mind.

"I got a hundred and forty seven dollars. We'll need gas."

Danny emerged from the gas station with milk, cookies, ham, cheese, and a loaf of bread.

"This will have to do for now. Got to watch the money."

"Buy me a pack of Salem's."

Danny didn't answer; a cold stare. Back on the highway.

"This van has probably been reported as stolen. That is, if it wasn't stolen when we got in it.," Loraine always thinking.

Danny was tuned out, thinking of the hammer of the revolver clicking behind his head. God saved him, a freak accident of nature. What if there is no God, what if there is?"

"What?" he answered.

"The van, Danny, it's probably stolen or reported stolen."

"Yeah?"

"Danny, snap out of it, you're not dead. We will be alright. God is with us. Trust Him, trust me, trust yourself."

"Yeah, you're right, it has to be that way, doesn't it?" Danny answered.

Modeena, busily fanning herself with an open hand, "Yeah it show do."

CHAPTER FORTY TWO

Modeena told Danny, "leave dat van down at the switch yard, I know someone dat take care of dat."

"Okay," Danny replied. "I'll see you tomorrow."

Modeena made her way into the dilapadated shack, brushing cob webs away from the door knob. "First things first," Modeena said aloud to herself..

She made her way through the house, making a bee line for the out house. Modeena reached for the jar stash. It was there, full of cash. That night she dug in the backyard unearthing twenty or more glass fruit jars. The jars lined the rickety old table, a single candle made counting the money easy and private.

Suddenly she felt a presence, then a shadow over her shoulder blocked the sole light. A large menacing figure stood before her as she turned.

"Cliff, you done scared me half to death."

"How much you got there Modeena?"

"I ain't done countin' it all. Two hundred thousand about all."

"I ditched the van, my men are taking it apart right about now. The parts will be in five states tomorrow."

"Dat's good work."

"Now what," Cliff asked.

"What Marie want?" Modeena quiered.

"She said she's retiring permanently and that you are her

replacement, you'll control the entire mid west operation, all the way to Chicago and back to Houston."

"What about the law down there, they's still after us?"

"No, never was. Marie had them paid off from the get go."

"No shit. Why she want me to shoot Mr. Danny and Loraine then?"

"That's Marie's way of having fun, giving someone a task that they're incapable of carrying out. She is a twisted sister alright."

"Charles I know would shoot they ass, mine too," Modeena declared with a forced grin.

"Yeah, Charles would, he's a dangerous man."

"Is he really FBI or do he belong to Maire?"

"Both," Cliff said.

"What's he gonna do?"

"He comes back here and runs the operation with you. Just like always, it's the biggest distribution center in the states now."

"You talked to Clara?" Modeena asked with a raised brow.

"I'll see her tonight, just as soon as Claude starts snoring," Cliff giggled.

"I swear you two is the baddest people I know," Modeena chuckled.

"Oh, there's just one more thing."

"What's dat?"

"Marie wanted me to ask you if you have a will?"

Modeena's eyes widened, her chuckle faded.

"Why dat?"

"You know why, we work in a dangerous business, that's all."

Nervously Modeena stammered, "Yeah, I got a will. All my money go to Mr. Danny and Bobby."

"Is that will here in one of those jars?"

"No, it ain't. It be in a safe place."

"Miss Clara wants to take a look at it. No need to fidget in your chair like that Modeena."

Cliff walked closer to the table calmly picking up the jar and tilting it to the side. Cliff poked out his lower lip.

"Hum, no will here?"

"No surh, show ain't."

"Miss Clara she gonna kill me?"

"No, who do you think is taking over for Marie- you?"

"No sur, no sur. I show knowed it ain't me."

"Clara set up this hub, it's her show, always has been."

"Marie's coming back to Mobile. Did you know that, with Charles?"

"No sur" Modeena stammered.

"Yeah, on your plane. You see Marie considers it a company plane. Furthermore she considers you an employee. Do you agree?"

"Yes sur, yes sur. I show do."

"Come up with your will, Marie and Clara want to see it."

"Okay" Modeena mumbled.

"By the way, don't leave this shack until Charles gets here tomorrow. He will be taking you back to the Bahamas for a while."

"Dat's so?"

"Yeah, dat's so, Modeena."

CHAPTER FORTY THREE

Meanwhile Danny and Loraine had walked the last two blocks from the switch yard. Home looked good, yet there was a distance Danny had never sensed. Danny rushed past Loraine the last few yards to the porch. He knocked on the door and peeked through the antique beveled glass in the door. Claude was coming to the door. Clara sat comfortably cross legged on the sofa in a hoochie mama nightie.

"My God, look who's here," Claude announced. The words were barcly out of his mouth when Danny grabbed Claude around the neck almost choking him with hugs.

Clara clamored upstairs returning in a long red terry cloth robe. Claude gave her a glance, shrugging. They gathered at the old yellow dinette set. Danny began the story, as Claude listened he recalled years ago. The red Plymouth wagon, the tires, his brain was churning. Clara listened intently, saying little. Danny would turn himself over to the U.S. authorities, after all, he was the victim, not the perpetrator. He knew it looked bad for him, his plane and all, actually Marie's.

"Are there warrants out for you in Argentina? Are you a wanted man?" Clara quizzed.

"I don't know."

"That's not the problem, the drug cartel people want us dead. We know to much."

"Really?" Clara continued. "What do you know?"

"That, that I was unknowingly smuggling drugs in the orphanage plane and that Marie knew it."

"So, are you saying Marie is a drug dealer?"

"No, I don't know."

"Modeena...." Danny caught himself, but not quick enough. Modeena's name had rolled off his tongue.

Clara seemed agitated. The conversation ended when Loraine said she was exhausted.

They retired for the night, but not before Danny pulled Claude aside. "Dad, I don't know we weren't followed. I'm paranoid and dog-tired. We left Modeena at her shack."

"Okay son, okay, I'll go over and check on her in the morning."

"Dad, that might be too late. That Charles she met at church is somehow connected to all this. Modeena thinks he is going to kill all of us."

"Get some rest, I'll go check on her, I'll wait until Clara's asleep. I have some things to tell you too."

Claude was restless, tossing and turning, subsequently he fell asleep. Clara hears her cue, the loud snoring, mouth ajar. She still donned her hoochie momma nightie, slapping on the red terry cloth robe she made her way downstairs and out the back door. Clara walked behind the detached garage. Cliff was waiting. Clara flashed her rope open, exposing the nightie. Cliff smiled. Clara let the robe fall.

Claude was dreaming. Danny was falling. He heard his body hit the ground hard, he was dead. Oh no, oh my God, no. Claude sprang upright in the bed. Was he talking in his sleep? His breathing was fast and painful. His morbid thoughts an abberation. Clara was gone. He looked for the light in the bathroom, it was out. Maybe she's downstairs. Wait, she's involved in all this. Maybe she's gone to Modeena's.

Claude found his gun and left the house silently. A figure appeared in the night. It was Clara.

"What are you doing out here?"

"I thought I heard something."

"Yeah, me too," Claude lied.

Clara made her way back inside the house. Claude walked toward

Modeena's shack. When he got to the switch yard he saw another figure, a man. He didn't look like a railroad man. Sweat pants and a jogger's top, a big fella. Claude made his way to Modeena's, he walked about some and saw no activity. She's alright, he thought and went home.

Next morning Claude stayed home to visit with Danny and Loraine. Clara declared she would be late tonight or tomorrow getting home. She was going to Mobile to see Marie, she had missed her. Danny was trying to make a doctor's appointment for Loraine, the baby was due any day.

Clara didn't go to Mobile. There was a gathering at Modeena's. Marie, Clara, Charles, Cliff and the local sheriff, a guy named Tadlock were there. It was not a planning session, today the plan will be executed. Marie was the matriarch; the others pawns to manipulate.

"Okay, one last time, we go over what each is to do." Marie ordered.

"Clara, go to the Bahamas with Modeena, get the money from our accounts. Modeena leave your money there if you want, just remember if you bring it back to the states a lot of questions will be raised. The IRS will want it's cut and proof of how you earned it. I advise against it, but it's your money, you earned it."

"Cliff you and Tadlock, are to take care of Clara's little problem. Charles you know what to do."

"Okay, today is retirement day for all of us."

Claude had a field to plow, Danny and Loraine found a doctor, the appointment was at one. "I'll just run out and plow while ya'll are gone, need to get it done before it rains."

"I understand Dad, do what you need to, we'll be alright."

Claude got to the field. He fired up the giant tractor with the huge wheels and let the bat wing plow sink into position. Claude thought best when he was on his tractor. He thought about how he met Clara, the dope or whatever it was in his tires. Modeena's wealth and her uncanny relationship with Clara. Could all that tie with Danny's troubles? Of course, it has to, Marie's a snake, a demon from hell. Orphanage or not."

A cop car approached, it was the sheriff, Tadlock. There's someone with him; no two, a guy in the front and one in the back seat.

"What the hell. I hope nothing bad has happened. An accident? Maybe Danny has been arrested?."

The men unloaded from the cop car, Claude pulled the tractor to a halt.

"What can I do for you sheriff?" Claude asked puzzled.

"You have the right to remain silent.." the sheriff went through the spill as he handcuffed Claude.

"What the hell are you doing? I haven't done anything!"

"How about harboring a fugitive?"

"You mean my son? He's innocent."

"Sit down" the sheriff barked and one of the other men brought the sheriff a pair of leg irons.

The large beefy man grabbed Claude easily dragging him to the front of the tractor. Charles had made his was to the cab of the tractor.

"Okay" Cliff shouted.

Claude was screaming, "My God, my God, what are you doing?"

Charles lowered the giant plow and gunned the beast right over Claude. He was killed instantly. Body parts were strewn for about ten feet.

The sheriff calmly went about retrieveing his restraints. One of the leg irons still attached to a leg severed just above the knee, a femur bone glistened from a tattered piece of denim.

"Okay" Cliff said. "Leave it in gear and the engine running, run it down to idle speed and kill the engine."

Charles did as he was directed, "Now be sure and turn the key back to the on position."

"Yeah, okay" Charles countered.

The murderers left, joking.

"Whew, that was a mess," Cliff grinned.

Now Clara was all his.

The sheriff chimed in, "Yeah, tragic these farm accidents are usually pretty gruesome."

Laughter filled the squad car as the sheriff dropped the two at their car.

The casket was closed since they had a problem finding all of Claude. Clara played the grieving widow to perfection. Modeena, Danny, Bobby and Loraine were distraught. Marie did not attend the funeral.

Clara was the sole heir in Claude's will, at least she thought she was. Claude had changed it to include Danny and Bobby; their share 50%. That was okay with her, after all she would need somebody to work the place. Her overall intention was not to profit from Claude's death rather than just enjoy it. He had served his purpose, Modeena was a sitting duck.

After an appropriate time six months or so she would marry Cliff. They would travel the world; maybe buy a villa on the French Rivera near Nice.

Clara's mind raced with visions of happiness. The dope business had been good to her. She just needed to tie up a few loose ends. Modeena was next. She knew too much, and was too careless in hiding her assets. Clara and Marie had joint and separate accounts in Switzerland and Germany. The loot was over a billion dollars.

Clara wanted Charles to "do" Modeena. Surprisingly Charles refused, saying, "I care for her." Clara told Cliff about it, they both had a big laugh. I suppose that's his way of saying he loves her. Cliff stopped laughing when Clara said he would have to do it. Cliff argued, "Look, I don't have the federal ace card Charles has. Get Tadlock to do it."

"No," Clara directed. "If you do it, I won't have to worry about you running off with some French cutie. Besides, our success has been based on taking care of problems ourselves. No outside hit man contracts. Too risky."

"Okay, when?" Cliff said, giving in to Clara's wishes.

"Soon, maybe a month or two."

Clara, Charles and Modeena went to the Bahamas just as Cliff said they would. Right after Claude's funeral. Modeena was terribly upset, little did she know Charles was the driver. Yet somehow she knew the accident wasn't an accident. She also knew Charles was a very dangerous man. Call it a sixth sense, hoo doo, whatever it was

Modeena had it. Her relationship with Charles was strained. She sure as hell didn't trust him. There was one way to find out how far he would go.

"Did you know Mr. Cliff asked me all about my will? He want me to take it to Marie and Clara."

"That so?" Charles said attentively.

"Yeah, they bees askin me who I be leaven my money to and all. Why you think they care about dat? Dey's gotz mo money dan me."

"Well..." Charles pondered. "That's an interesting question. I wish you had told me about that. I mean sooner than now."

"What you think?:"

Charles was silent, walking back and forth, he looked troubled.

After a minute Modeena said, "Charles, what you think?"

"I think you and I are next." Charles said in a low voice.

"Me too, datz exactly what gonna happen."

"Only one thing we can do, get them first," Charles said with a stern face.

"Oh Lord, I can't be doin none of dat, selling dem drugs is one thang. But the Lord knows I can't be doin dat. I'd be in hell I know for show. Fooling Mr. Danny and Loraine like we don datz okay, but we was almost kilt by dat crazy Mexican. I be wantin' dem back here too. But I ain't havin nothin' to do with killin' nobody."

"Look Modeena, it's part of the business; drugs, murder, corruption, it's you or them."

"No it ain't. Miss Clara done told me when she took me in, dese plants, dese drugs comes from is God's creation. She told me Indians smokes um, eats um, has for hundreds of years. Ought to be they business, not da governments."

"Modeena, it's a lot more complicated than that. It's big money, big time players. They aren't going to let us out. They know where to find us."

"Well, let's find dem first, but we ain't killin' nobody!"

The phone rang. It was Danny. "We have a baby girl!" his voice was as excited as he could muster.

"We was just talkin' about comin' to Mississippi. I got to see dat girl. We ain't never had no girl, praise the Lord."

Charles and Modeena walked into the same maternity ward where Danny and Bobby were born. In no time Modeena had the baby in her arms. Charles surprisingly also took an interest, taking his turn holding the baby.

"Clara's coming, she was here yesterday."

"Oh yeah?" Modeena's manly voice rising higher.

"You named dis baby?"

"No, not yet. We're thinking about Mary, maybe Mary Jo."

"Oh, dat sound coote. You know somebody named Mary?"

Loraine was quick, "Mary, mother of God."

"Oh yeah, oh yeah, I knows dat."

"You should know it, I was praying to her to answer our prayers... you know, when we were on our knees."

"Yeah, I show do."

Clara walked through the door. Modeena looked up and without thinking said, "Where's Cliff?"

"Who's Cliff?" Danny and Loraine said in unison. There was a strained silence. Then Clara managed a quick, no so convincing, lie.

"He's my new driver."

"I didn't know you had a driver, you always enjoyed driving, sometimes you would put the top down and stay gone for hours." Danny said.

"Well, I got one now, let me see that baby."

Clara practically yanked her from Modeena's arms, giving her an awful stare in the process.

Danny had a strong gut feeling something was terribly wrong with what he had just heard. There was another man—of course. Dad would never fall out of a tractor, he was too careful. I didn't believe it when they told me. Something is terribly, terribly wrong.

Danny sat a moment, then sprang from the room.

"Danny, Danny," Loraine sang out.

Clara glared at Modeena, she mouthed the words but didn't speak them, "You stupid bitch!"

Loraine perplexed, continued looking at the door for Danny's return.

CHAPTER FORTY FOUR

The baby was crying. Loraine was up and about quicker than most, apparently she was made for having kids. Danny paced the floor when he was home. His Dad's death and the circumstances were troubling. He sold the tractor that killed Claude, it was too much to bear to even look at it. When cleaning out the tool box he found Claude's pistol. He kept asking himself why it would be there. Dad must have expected trouble. Then why didn't he use it to defend himself? Maybe I got him killed, the drug dealers would kill me not him. This just doesn't make sense.

Modeena and Charles hung around a day or two staying at the DeMoss house. There was a certain irony in the fact that the visitor was Claude's killer. If Modeena knew it, she would kill Charles herself. But the problem now was to keep Clara and Cliff from killing them. Bobby and Clara moped around in a depressed state, of course, Clara's was an act. Cliff, had orders from Clara to stay away. She would contact him to make arrangements to kill Modeena and Charles. Cliff, had convinced her to let someone else do it.

Cliff, boarded the plane to New Orleans. There he would find a man for the job. Clara had decided to make it look like a lover's triangle. So the lucky bastard chosen would soon be departing to hell.

Cliff, got a cab to the lower south side. There were hoards of drug addicts and evil elements working there. The cab driver let him out at a predominately black barbeque restaurant. Cliff, had heard of it as a real good place to eat, if you wanted to risk you life for a pulled pork sandwich. The driver offered some advise as Cliff paid the fare, "Mister, you better get your food to go. Dis here be a bad neighborhood."

"I'm big enough to take care of myself," Cliff boasted.

"Yes, sir, you big enough, but down here you just a bigger target."

Cliff smirked.

"Okay, I done told you." the driver warned. The yellow cab disappeared into a golden sunset.

Cliff ordered the ribs, a young black man served him. The do-rag and swaggering walk let Cliff know it would be a safe bet to talk.

"Say, I'm looking for a man about forty years old to do a job for me."

Lester's name tag looked out of place on his sauce stained t-shirt.

"Mister, don't no black men live to be forty down here."

Cliff grabbed the young man's arm and snatched his one hundred forty pound body so the boys face was very close to his.

"I didn't come down here for bullshit, friend."

Lester never lost his coolness. "Robbery or homicide?"

"I need a bad man, badder than me."

"What's in it for me?" Lester replied.

"A nice tip, it'll be right under this plate when I finish my ribs."

"Cool," Lester flashed back.

"I'll be here tomorrow, you workin'?"

"Yeah," the cocky little man replied.

Back in Elmbrook Danny had come up with a plan to see where Clara was going, who she was seeing. A private eye and the local cops were not options. It was obvious to Danny . He'd fly around when she took her little trips. He'd seen plenty from the air."

Claude's life insurance wasn't much, his assets were the farm and a little cash. Danny would get forty thousand after his split with Bobby. Enough to buy a J-3 Cub, it could go slow enough to keep track of her from the air.

Danny looked around and found one in Florida, He would have Loraine drive him down, he'd keep it in the barn at the farm. Clara hadn't been out there in years. Bobby asked to tag along, he'd ridden a few times with Danny and liked flying. They left the following morning, drove all day and stayed in a twenty dollar a night flea bag motel. The baby didn't seem to mind, if she started to cry, Loraine would let her nurse even if she wasn't hungry.

Danny liked the plane; cheap enough, five thousand, a local doctor's play pretty. Danny took the plane for a trip or two around the airport, checking it out, landing and taking off twice. It had a fresh overhaul, was neat as a pin, the good doctor had a pair of headsets so the guy in front could talk to the guy in the seat directly behind him. A nice bonus Danny thought.

Danny and Bobby climbed in and took off. He'd circle Loraine in the car below, checking out his air surveillance theory. Doing slow S curves above her. Danny, for the first time, was not thinking about his Dad and the others. He was simply enjoying his new plane, a cheap, slow 1940's throw back, but it was his.

"Danny?"

"Yeah Bobby."

"Let me fly it."

"Okay. Keep her steady and level, don't do anything quick or jerky, Okay?" Danny instructed. Danny couldn't help but think of Federico and the emphatic hand signals.

"Watch your airspeed and altitude."

"Yeah, okay."

They flew for ten minutes or so, Bobbie's first pilot experience.

"Danny, I been wanting to talk to you."

"Yeah, about what?"

"About Mom."

"Okay, talk."

"Well," a short pause in his voice. "I think she had something to do with Dad's accident."

Danny, soundless, the hair stood on the back of his neck. How would Bobby know? He's just a kid.

"Why do you think that?"

"Well, you know down on Wellington Street there's concrete sidewalks and that overpass above the switch yards."

"Yeah, go on."

"I was skateboarding down there and was walking back over the overpass. I saw Mom, some big man. They were kissing. Then the sheriff's car came up. Charles was in it with Sheriff Tadlock. Then the big guy got in the car. That was the same day Dad died."

Danny was dead quiet.

"Don't you think that's strange? Mom kissing another guy, then..."

Danny interrupted him, "Wait, wait a minute, I've got to think."

"Danny, I don't want to fly anymore."

"Okay, let go of the stick and take your feet off the pedals."

Danny could tell Bobby was upset.

Danny turned and headed back to check on Loraine. Wheels were turning in his head. Sounds like the same setup as Argentina, bad cops, pay off, no doubt. But this time Clara instead of Marie.

"Bobby?"

"Yeah, Danny."

"You told anybody else about this?"

"No"

"You sure?"

"Yeah."

Listen to me very carefully. Don't tell anyone, I mean anyone about this. Okay?"

"Okay Danny."

The hopscotch across the country side ended. Bobby helped Danny get the plane in the barn. Loraine picked them up.

"What's wrong? Danny you're trembling. Is it the plane?"

"No," Danny replied looking at Bobby, "tell Loraine what you told me."

"But you told me not to tell anyone."

"Just tell it. But remember never tell it to anyone else. Not even the police, Okay?"

"Yeah, Danny." Bobby told it again to Loraine. Danny listened carefully. Seeing if Bobby varied his story in the slightest. He did not, telling it exactly the same.

Bobby was crying by the end of the second telling.

Danny asked, "What's wrong?"

"Will Mom go to jail?"

"No, she won't." Danny answered, not really knowing anything else to say.

Danny and Loraine looked at each other, there was sorrow upon sorrow in the look. They drove to the empty DeMoss house, Clara had not returned. Later that evening Clara called, she'd decided to stay in Mobile a few more days.

CHAPTER FORTY FIVE

Marie, Cliff, and Clara would take care of Modeena and Charles. In order to do so they would have to regain their trust. The retirement and good life with plenty of money had to look real. In a month or two without any problems, all would be relaxed. Cliff, had the man from New Orleans waiting. With Modeena gone Clara could relax, not have to worry about her shooting off her mouth without thinking like she did in the maternity ward. Not have to worry about lavish spending drawing too much attention from the authorities in the Bahamas. That would be entirely possible. Clara could fix it, like always, pay offs. Every cop has his price was her favorite saying. It had served Marie well. Clara had thought it through. Modeena would die. Charles too. He was just too dangerous and unpredictable.

Marie would be eighty- two in a month. Clara called Modeena. "We're planning a birthday celebration for Marie. Can you and Charles come?"

Modeena covered the phone and looked at Charles. "Can we go to Mobile for Marie's birthday party?"

"No, No Charles said we have plans here. A big real estate deal, we bought a high rise condo building right on the beach. We'll be busy with that."

Modeena recounted the true story, at least about buying the building, to Clara.

"Great" Clara said, "We'll just have it in the Bahamas. Next month on May 23, look for a party. I will send some people in advance to arrange it. Bye now."

"I swear dat woman show changed since I first met her. She mo like Marie every day," Modeena said.

Charles got the words out of his mouth as soon as Modeena put the phone on the receiver, "They are gonna hit us, I know it."

"What we gonna do Charles?"

"Have the party, it's on our turf, that's always an advantage."

Clara stayed in Mobile, never returning to Elmbrook. That suited Danny fine, he loved Bobby, Loraine and little Mary Jo. Clara would call once or twice a week with same lame excuses why she couldn't return just yet. They all knew she was with the 'big man', possibly Claude's killer. Thinking of her began to repulse Danny, he felt pity for Bobby knowing Clara's genetic composition was in his gene pool. Of course, he never mentioned it to Bobby. He would find out soon enough after high school biology.

The invitations came in the afternoon mail. Modeena would send her plane to Mobile for the DeMoss clan on the 22nd of May. Danny accepted, he missed Modeena and wanted to see her. He wondered if Bobby would be able to identify the big man.

Charles and Modeena met the plane in the limo. The first thing Modeena did was go after the baby. Loraine hesitantly gave her up. The more she and Danny had talked the more Loraine had come to realize that Modeena's religion was not genuine. A dogmatic obsession of quotes from scripture. Poorly understood and never practiced in reverence. An act cut from the same cloth as Clara's. Or was it?

Modeena held the baby as they rode.

"See that building over there? It's mine. That's where we're having the party. The three top stories are reserved. It's one of the tallest buildings on the island."

Danny noticed it right off. Modeena's diction and dialect were different. This wasn't the Modeena he grew up with, maybe living with Charles had changed her. Being one of the most articulate people Danny had ever met.

The party began and rolled into the night. There were at least two hundred people attending, the top floor reserved for the guest of honor and her closest friends and family.

Among the guests a hired killer to "do" Modeena. Clara, Marie and Charles retired to a small balcony for some privacy. Cliff and the man from New Orleans came to join them. It was windy so the little impromptu meeting would be quick and painless. They showed the man a picture of Modeena taken with a Polaroid that same evening. "Make sure he's got the right person. Oh yeah, pay him." Clara said to Cliff.

The party was getting louder. Loud enough no one could over hear what was being said.

"You got the money?" Marie asked Cliff.

"Yeah, it's right here."

"Pay the man," Marie said.

"All of it." Cliff answered.

"Yeah, why not. Because where we're going... he's not going to spend it."

Marie leaned over and moved a small potted plant. Exposing what appeared to be a small black box with a plunger in the top. Red wires were running over the side of the balcony.

Cliff, looked closer, trying to figure out what it was. Marie pushed the plunger home. There were two loud cracks, like fire crackers.

Everyone looked alarmed. Charles, the most intelligent, made a move to the open doorway, a yard or two away. Being trained in explosives he knew what he had heard. That was enough movement to start the collapse. Clara screamed at Marie, "You crazy old bitch!"

The balcony gave way like the hinges on a piano seat. It hung temporarily. Cliff, went over the rail, grabbing at air. In a desperate lunge he grabbed the railing. That was enough, just enough to cause the beams to separate from the structure.

The aftermath was horrific. Five bodies bludgeoned beyond recognition by the concrete upon impact. Cliff, actually exploded like a water balloon. Clara skewed through the middle by a lawn chair, Charles was face down when rolled over he was faceless. The New Orleans man hit so hard it blew both his laced up shoes off. Marie landed face up still clutching her birthday Bloody Mary glass.

Danny and the rest went home, funerals were held. Days turned to months.

One day a man called and said he had something to discuss with Danny.

Modeena arranged a meeting that same night when Danny got home from the farm.

The man began, "I'm the attorney for the late Marie LaSalle. She has left you and your minor brother Bobby her entire estate. I might add. It's more than substantial. There is a condition however, you are to donate enough money to run an orphanage in Argentina for the duration of you and your brother's lives. Also, your daughter and any additional children that should be born to you receiving any amount of said inheritance, will also continue the donations.

   Is that agreed?"

"Why yes, yes it is," Danny said, smiling.

"How much is the estate?"

"Around two billion dollars, give or take a million or two. And of course, my fee."

The man left. He pulled out onto Wellington Street. There was a political sign left over from the May election. It read:

Re-elect Tadlock.

for Sheriff

4th Term

The End